The Gray Between Us

Alona Simonsen

ISBN
Hardbound-978-621-495-155-0
MOBI/KINDLE-978-621-495-156-7
Softbound/Paperback-978-621-495-157-4

Cover illustration by:
Deudonne Mireo 'Rio' Orpia

Published by:
Poetry Planet Book Publishing House
Rosario, Pozorrubio, Pangasinan, Philippines
Contact Number: 09554960044

This is a work of fiction. Names, characters, businesses, events and incidents are the products of the author's imagination. Any resemblance to actual persons, living or dead, or actual events is purely coincidental.

For my husband, our son
And for my mother

Table of Contents

\

Erika feels the serene emotion suddenly enveloping her as she continues talking with Anthony.

"I haven't decided yet, or at least it is not yet final. For now, all I can say is that I am in the middle of the crossroads."

Erika hears Anthony sigh. This only means that something is bothering him.

Erika hears Anthony continues on the other line, "I emailed a poem to you last night. I can't sleep after I read your letter and poem. As I have said, your poem and letter made me reflect and contemplate. At the same time, you are inspiring me."

What can I say?

You inspired me too!

That's what Erika wants to say, but instead she says, "Thank you. I am humbled."

I am humbled.

What kind of reply was that?

Erika wants to kick herself.

Here she goes again!

She feels like a weirdo when she is talking with Anthony.

Where is the loquacious Erika?

Erika is calm earlier, but she realizes now that her calm is in a temporary hibernation.

The Gray between Us

Chapter 1

A dusk of pale tangerine
Envelopes us as we sit
Staring right at the horizon
Filled with unspoken emotion

It is the first Saturday of May, and Erika wakes up so early. Erika should still be sleeping by now. It is finally summer vacation, and there are no classes to stress about.

But it is not Erika's usual Saturday morning, because today she will meet Anthony after so many years of not seeing him.

Erika looks at her mobile phone for the nth time since she agreed on going out.

Yes! It is today!

Anthony will be waiting for her at the Buendia bus terminal in Manila.

"Why am I so nervous?" Erika asks herself.

Since they planned this meeting a couple of weeks ago, Erika was so nervous that she couldn't concentrate so much.

She wonders how she was able to study for her exams and finish all her reports at the same time, given her frame of mind.

Erika is currently studying law in The Law School in Taft Avenue, Manila. She just finished her first year and is finally thinking of relaxing at home.

She doesn't need to travel for a while. It is not easy for her to study law on weekends while working full-time on weekdays.

But becoming a lawyer has always been her dream. To realize her dream, Erika took a Bachelor of Arts with a major in economics at Calamba University or CU, as a preparatory course. She soon landed a job as a financial analyst/business planner in an industrial company in Sta. Rosa, Laguna, right after she graduated. And when the opportunity knocked to combine working and studying law, she grabbed it without a second glance.

And today, she will be traveling back again to Manila for a different reason. Erika smiles as she remembers a funny incident after Anthony sent her a message.

Anthony asked her if they could meet.

They planned to watch a movie and stroll around. For the past four years, they seldom talk. That was after Erika and Anthony went in different directions and chased their own dreams. Anthony called her and sent her text messages a few times during those years.

And then silence.

Erika doesn't remember how long that silence between them was. She just knew that it was deafening.

So, receiving a text message asking if they can meet after years of not seeing each other is wreaking havoc on her sanity.

She typed a message to her best friend, Loris.

Loris and Erika were classmates in college for four years. She knew the whole story about Erika and Anthony. She witnessed how the friendship between Erika and Anthony blossomed over the years, even after they parted ways right after graduation.

Erika is more of a serious type, while Loris is very bubbly. Being with her best friend is a source of joy to Erika.

Always!

Hei, guess what? Anthony and I will meet. 1st sat of May. I can't believe it! I'm so freaking excited!

The funny thing was that instead of sending the message to Loris, as she intended, she sent it to Anthony!

OMG!

Can I unsend the message?

She blushed tremendously, and she felt her face warmed up with shame even if no one saw her at that time.

Erika remembered that she prayed so hard that day. She asked the heavens that her text message wouldn't come through—that, if possible, the message would go directly to the clouds somewhere, so Anthony would not be able to receive it.

Erika waited for a reply for days about the message, but she didn't get any.

She thought that maybe her prayer had been heard.

"Your breakfast is ready! Don't go without eating first," Erika hears her mother say.

This breaks her line of thought about the text message incident.

"Yes, mom. I will go shower first," replies Erika.

She is so lucky.

Her mother is always taking care of her, even if she herself is a grown woman and can take care of herself. But her mother single-handedly raised her alone after her father died when she was still six years old.

Even up to now, her mother has been doing what she

usually does since Erika can remember, and that is taking care of her even if she doesn't have to.

Erika takes a shower and then puts on her clothes. She eats the breakfast her mother has prepared for her. When she's done, Erika hurries. Traffic is very unpredictable, especially during the summer.

Calamba in Laguna is a popular swimming destination in the country because of the many private and public pools in the area. Many local tourists from different neighboring cities and regions visit the place to relax, swim, and cool down.

Los Baños, where Erika lives, is a neighboring town to Calamba. Traveling to Manila will only mean that Erika will pass through all the traffic points within the area.

At around nine o'clock, Erika is finally on her seat inside an air-conditioned bus and on her way to Manila. As expected, there is already traffic.

It is ok.

She still has time, and hopefully the traffic is only around the Calamba area.

Traffic and the scourging heat are giving commuters like her a terrible travel experience. That is why it's always a better choice for her to take the air-conditioned bus, even if the fare is a lot more expensive than the ordinary.

Her phone vibrates, and Erika hears a ding with an incoming text message as the bus passes by the street going to CU. It is from Anthony!

Erika smiles at Anthony's impeccable timing. She takes out her mobile phone and reads the message.

Hei. Good morning ☺
Are you still home or on your way?

Good morning to you, too.

Erika mumbles to herself while grinning.

She looks to her left to see if the other passenger, the lady sitting beside her, notices her grinning alone. The lady beside her is busy with her own phone.

Thank goodness for that.

She then replies to Anthony's text.

Hei and good morning to you, too.
I am in the bus now. I will text you later
when we are in Alabang.

Before she even sets her mobile phone down, another text message arrives.

Ok. I'll wait for it then. See you soon ☺

Erika didn't reply. She will just text him, as she said, when the bus is at Alabang. She can't help but reminisce about the times when she and Anthony became friends.

They were both graduating college students in CU. She was an economics student, while Anthony was taking up psychology. Both courses were in the Arts and Sciences (A/S) Department. The department was located on the third floor of the main building.

They used to see each other in passing, either in the corridor going to their respective classes or when there were activities at school.

However, they never really "talked" to each other, except in their last year.

In the first semester of Erika's last year at the university, she had the 'Life and Works of Heroes' subject. And so does Anthony.

This subject focused on the lives and works of different heroes in the country. Since Dr. Jose P. Rizal, the Philippines national hero, was born in Calamba, Laguna, they used to visit his house called 'Bahay ni Rizal' or Rizal Shrine. This is where he lived as a child, and therefore they used to visit the place as part of their studies.

This practical approach aims to help them better understand some historical facts about his childhood.

Even during their visit, they wore their CU uniform. Erika wore a white blouse with a thin red lining and a navy-blue pleated skirt.

While it was a white polo shirt with the university logo on the upper right side and black pants for Anthony. Both of them wore black shoes.

It was during this visiting time that they first started to talk. Especially when Erika and Anthony were paired together during the area assignments in the shrine.

They were tasked to write a narrative report about the 'wishing well' and its significance in the hero's childhood.

This was the time they got to know one another. This gave Erika and Anthony time to talk to each other.

Their common topics were their own impression of Mt. Makiling, student life in CU, OJT, research, as well as their dreams, among others.

CU is located on twenty hectares of land. The main building is castle-inspired, made more beautiful by a wide green field and Mt. Makiling as a backdrop.

It is simply majestic!

At the last day of their visit at Rizal Shrine, Erika and Anthony visited also the old Catholic Church that is just located on the other side of Rizal Shrine.

They also went to the little park on the other side with a giant clay pot they called 'banga', which serves as the City's landmark.

As days and weeks passed, the communication between them became closer and more open. Erika told Anthony that she took economics as a preparatory course for her dream.

She wanted to be a lawyer, and she was thinking that if time and budget permitted, one day she would be one. That's why Erika was active in the student council. She was, in fact, vice president of the Arts and Sciences student council that year.

Anthony, on the other hand, was one of the editors of The University Publication, the official newspaper of the university.

Erika learned from Anthony that he was from the Bicol region. He studied and graduated from high school at the University of Legazpi (UL) in Albay.

He has relatives in Laguna and decided to try it here after high school.

As weeks went by, they haven't had time to see each other as often as they want to.

They are both busy with all the requirements they need to finish.

As a graduating student, Erika was busy all the time. Aside from her research paper, she also had on-the-job training (OJT) in an electronics company in Carmelray Industrial Park 1 in Canlubang, which is still part of Calamba.

Even if it's a bit far from CU, they had shuttle buses that made the travel back and forth easier; not to mention, Erika saved money.

Erika had many extracurricular activities, such as being a pioneer and active member of the Youth Ministry Group and a volunteer in the outreach program of the university.

Sometimes Erika wondered how she was able to accomplish everything.

So, Erika knew that it was tough for Anthony to find time to always send a message or meet her.

But when he did find time, Anthony used to send emails just to say hello or tell her what he was up to.

That's what she likes about Anthony.

Subject: just saying hi

Dear Erika,

Hi! That's all. Just kidding!

So, how's your day so far? I hope it's good.

Well, I am, if you will ask. I am doing fine. I am just busy writing my research papers and preparing for the visit of the image of the Virgin Mary. I will be covering it for the university publication.

Hope to see you during the vigil. ☺

Anthony

"Mani, popcorn, shingaling, tubig, ice tea!" a man selling food and drinks shouts in the bus.

Erika hears him, and this momentarily pierces her memory of how she and Anthony became friends.

The bus is going so slowly.

It is almost ten o'clock already, and they are still in Crossing, Calamba. There are many passengers already standing inside the bus, as well as sellers of food and drinks trying to earn a little.

It will be a long journey.

She buys a bottle of ice-cold tea.

After sipping a bit, she thinks that the tea tastes weird. With a shake of her head, she almost laughs as another memory creeps into her mind.

Weird tasting ice tea!?

Huh! I heard this phrase before.

Or rather, she had read it from Anthony's email before.

This was right after he visited her in the student council office.

She gave Anthony a glass of iced tea and chocolate-chip cookies.

After he ate the cookies and drank the tea, he had been

grinning all the time, to the point that it annoyed her.

She asked him what the matter was, but he never said a thing that time.

"What's wrong? Why do you look like that?"

"Huh? How do I look?"

"Your expression is a bit different. You are grinning from ear to ear."

Anthony didn't answer but smiled so wide. He then looked at his watch and said that he must go.

"I will send you a message tonight. I just have to rush now. We have a meeting in about five minutes."

Anthony just said that and hurried to the door.

He sent her an email that evening, as he promised.

Subject: Hello

Erika,

It was nice seeing you today.

Sorry that I couldn't stay that long earlier. I need to finish the article due tomorrow. I just want to see you and say hello.

By the way, thank you for the cookies and the weird-tasting ice tea.

See you when I see you. ☺

Anthony

Erika laughed after reading the email.

She was wondering why and how the ice tea tasted weird. It was just ordinary ice tea.

Huh!?!

Maybe it was not the iced tea that was weird.

Maybe it was Anthony.

Reading his message that evening thrilled her, and she couldn't figure out why. Erika was bothered by the thrilling sensation in a good way. All of these are new to her.

This is normal, isn't it?

Erika shook her head.

No! No! No!

It can't be!

We are just friends. It seems wrong and too soon!

She silently mumbled.

Erika knew then that she was in trouble.

Chinito trouble!

Chapter 2

"Miss, where will you get off?" the bus conductor asks her.

He's holding a bunch of tickets and a puncher. The conductor is waiting for Erika's answer.

Erika is a little bit confused, but she recovers and says, "Buendia."

After punching holes in the ticket, the conductor gives it to Erika and collects the bus fare, then he moves on to the next passenger.

Erika puts the ticket in her sling bag. She looks outside to see where they are now.

Still in Crossing.

Still a long way to go.

She just closes her eyes and continues her reminiscing.

It was the month of January on her last year in college, when Erika participated in the Youth Festival. She was one of the participants from CU. She was so excited because she's never been to the Bicol region, most especially in Legazpi, Albay.

University of Legazpi (UL) hosted that year's festival. Delegations from different schools, colleges, and universities all over the country participated in the festival.

It was a four-day event, and the collegiate publication chose Anthony as their representative. His tasks were to document the event and write a news article about it, as well as participate in different programs at the festival.

The CU delegations were in one bus going to Legazpi.

Standing inside the UL campus, Erika thought that it was so big, just like CU, if not bigger. It is very beautiful, too.

If CU has Mt. Makiling, UL has Mt. Mayon.

From where Erika was staying during the festival, she could see the perfect cone shape of the amazing Mayon volcano.

Yes.

Mt. Mayon is a volcano. And in fact, it is one of the active volcanoes in the Philippines.

It is a popular destination for local and international tourists because of its perfect symmetrical cone shape. Being able to see Mt. Mayon with her very own eyes was one of the reasons why Erika was so excited about this trip to the Bicol region.

She also had the opportunity to visit the famous Cagsawa Ruins in Daraga, Albay. The place is also famous because it offers a better view of Mt. Mayon.

That's why Erika took her chances of having her picture taken with the iconic view of Mt. Mayon and the remnants of the church ruins in one frame.

She even bought a souvenir gray-colored t-shirt with the Cagsawa Ruins and Mt. Mayon print design in front.

It was during their stay in Legazpi that Erika realized that she was developing a deeper feeling for Anthony.

Is it because of the beautiful surroundings?

It was just nice to see Anthony in his hometown, in a place where he grew up, plus the magic of Mayon. Well, Erika felt a kind of spell enveloping her while she was looking at the volcano.

On their third day of the festival, they went on a pilgrimage in Tiwi, Albay.

This activity took half a day as they went to the 'holy place' by foot. It was very calming for her because, as they walked on the mountainside, Erika could see the sea waves splashing right below. The cold, fresh air was like a hug, enveloping her senses as she walked towards their destination.

This chill made her feel the peacefulness of the area, the happiness of the people, and the simplicity of life in Albay. She felt lighter as she continued her journey together with the other festival delegates.

She felt at home.

During the pilgrimage, she was looking all around to see where Anthony was. She didn't see him. Thinking he must be busy writing an article about the festival, she didn't bother to continue looking for him.

On their way back to UL, after the pilgrimage was over, delegates who wanted to buy "pasalubongs" or something they could take back home, could do so.

Since Bicol region is known for *pili nuts*, sometimes called 'java almonds', and Albay has an abundance of pili, Erika bought different pili products like brittles and tarts for Loris.

She also bought a couple of bottles of native *laing*.

Laing is a popular Filipino dish from the Bicol region. This dish is made of taro leaves with either meat or seafood and cooked in thick coconut milk or cream. It is usually spiced up with chili, garlic, ginger, lemongrass, shrimp paste, and onions. Her mother likes this dish she calls 'tipay'.

As for her, Erika bought a native abaca bag in its natural honey color, handcrafted in the area.

Erika and the rest of the CU delegations went to the presentation night right after the pilgrimage.

Everyone must participate in the dance number that the team has selected. Erika had no idea who chose the song for their presentation number. She didn't have a choice, though; she danced to the music like everybody else in the group.

After the program, they all went back to their respective rooms. Erika was sharing a room with another three ladies from their delegation. She started packing all her belongings so they would be ready the next day. They would all go back home to Laguna after the festival is over.

Erika went out of the room to enjoy the fresh air of the night right after she was done packing her things.

At the far end of the corridor, Erika saw Anthony sitting on a chair facing Mt. Mayon.

Erika noticed that Anthony usually chose to be alone. There were times, too, when he seemed to be in deep thought.

Sometimes, right after their group session, he would find a place to sit down with a piece of paper in front of him and a pen in his hand.

She decided to walk towards him anyway. He was busy writing on a piece of orange-colored paper.

Erika recognized the orange-colored paper. It was a leaflet from the festival.

"Hey, stranger! What are you doing?"

"Oh, hey there! I am writing a poem, but I can't seem to finish. I don't know. I can't find the right words."

Erika looked down at the paper and saw a few stanzas

of the poem without a title.

"Ok. I should leave you in peace, then. I hope you can finish that poem. See you in the morning."

And Anthony smiled in reply to Erika.

Erika waved her hand and went back to her room.

There was a nagging feeling she couldn't shy away from, and she couldn't explain it either. Erika thought that Anthony seemed different in his hometown, and he was very much in deep thought most of the time.

Maybe he just missed his life in Legazpi.

The next day, before they traveled back to Laguna, Anthony gave Erika the leaflet he used the night before to write the poem.

"I was not able to finish the poem. Can you keep it for me, please?" Anthony asked Erika with a smile.

"Am I allowed to read it?" Erika replied.

Anthony smiled and said, "Of course."

They went inside the bus and took their separate seats. Erika wanted to read the 'not finish' poem, so she opened the leaflet right away.

As the bird hums in the distance
And the stars shine above us
I can feel all my emotions
Swinging in just one direction

As I look at the perfect cone-shape
Of my hometown's majestic mountain
I can clearly picture you in my head
And how you make me dazzled

As the clouds touch and kiss

...

It was such a lovely short poem.

It made Erika wonder about the inspiration behind this poem and why Anthony was not able to finish it.

Who could probably make Anthony dazzled?

Maybe one day I will know.

She was hoping that Anthony would be able to finish the poem one day!

She took out her phone from her bag and started typing a text message to Anthony.

Your poem is very visual and poetic
at the same time. I like it very much. ☺

She then pressed the send button.

Not long after, her phone 'dinged' again. Erika saw an immediate reply from Anthony.

Thank you. I wish I was able to finish,
though. ☺

Instead of texting back, Erika looked back to where Anthony was sitting. She waved and smiled at him.

Anthony smiled brightly in return.

The trip back to Laguna might be long, but she was not sleepy at all. Erika stayed awake the whole time, even if almost everyone in the bus was already sleeping. She was just looking outside and looking at the green scenery. It was as if Erika was trying to save everything she was seeing and feeling in her memory.

And for the last time, she wanted to see the majestic Mt. Mayon.

In her mind, she doesn't know if or when she would be able to go back to this place.

Along the way, Erika felt that she had left a part of her heart in the Bicol region, specifically in Albay.

A week had already passed since they returned from Bicol, but Erika hadn't seen Anthony. She hadn't gotten any text or email messages from him, and she wondered why.

She doesn't want to ask either.

He will text me or send me a message if he wants to or if he has time.

Erika reasoned out.

She got her answer when they saw each other in the main lobby. Erika was on her way to the chapel, coming directly from the guidance office, which was located on the right side of the lobby's entrance.

Anthony, on the other hand, came from the library and was already on his way out.

"Hey. It's good to see you again, Erika," greeted Anthony.

"Hey. Likewise! You are becoming a stranger these days," replied Erika.

"I know, and I'm sorry. I really do." Anthony smiled and scratched his head.

Anthony explained to Erika that he was not on campus

due to his research. The University Publication also tasked him with covering the different sports events in Southern Tagalog held at PH College the week before.

"I was just kidding. I know how busy you are. Anyway, I have been busy myself, too," said Erika in reply to Anthony.

"I went to the council office last time, but you were not there. I was in a hurry because my research group was waiting for me. I just wanted to see you and say hello." Anthony told her.

"You were? I didn't know." Erika didn't know that Anthony dropped by the council office to see her.

Nobody had mentioned it to her.

"Maybe I will not be able to visit you in the office for a while from now because I have lots of things to do and assignments to finish. I will try, though."

Well, what can she do?

She's busy too!

"I understand, Anthony. Just don't be a stranger, will you?" Erika said.

"Of course not! And hey, I miss you, Erika." Anthony replied,

Erika didn't reply to that.

She wanted to say she missed him too, but she didn't have the courage to say it.

After another week, Erika began to feel uneasy.

She missed Anthony, his smile, and his jokes. Even if she didn't want to admit it, not even to herself, there was no point in denying it.

No one visited her in the council office anymore, and

this made Erika a bit sad.

Erika felt pathetic for being sad.

She wanted to text him, but she was shy about texting him first. Erika usually just replies to Anthony's message, not the other way around.

I will just wait, she told herself.

A day after Valentine's Day, Erika opened her email and found a message from Anthony.

I guess he's not busy!

She's sitting alone in front of a computer in the student council office, reading the email.

Most of the council officers were in their respective classes.

Subject: Hello

Dear Erika,

Well, I just wanted to say hello. How's your "balentayms"? Did you go out on a date? I hope not.

Just kidding, or not!

I got chocolate bars from Juris. I would save some for you. I haven't seen you in ages. I hope everything is well with you.

Good luck in your final thesis defense. I will have mine in two days.

Wish me luck!

Anthony

Erika replied to Anthony. But instead of an email message, she just sent him a text.

Hey. I've read your message. I had a date
yesterday, fyi. And how about you?
Btw, good luck to your defense.

Erika went out with Loris the day before, and she didn't mention that to Anthony. It didn't really count as a 'date', especially for what Anthony might have had in mind when he asked Erika. She just wanted to find out what his reaction would be.

She was just smiling, thinking about it.

And not long after Erika sent the message, her mobile phone vibrated, and her favorite song "Breathless" from the singing group The Corrs started playing.

It has always been her ringing tone since she got her phone for the first time. She didn't want to change it—not yet anyway.

Anthony is calling....

This was what was flashing on her phone screen as Erika answered the phone.

"Hello"

"Hey. So, you had a date on Valentine's Day. Do I know him? Or are you just kidding me?" Anthony asked Erika without preamble.

"Gotcha!" answered Erika while laughing.

Anthony laughed, too, and said, "You made me sweat there for a while. I thought you really had a date with some guy. I know I don't have the right to feel this way, but I felt blindsided and nervous."

"Huh?! Why was that?" Erika asked.

"I don't know. I feel so close to you that I thought if there's someone lurking around, I would know." Anthony answered.

"You will tell me, right?" he continued.

Erika said, "Of course!"

She then told Anthony that she was out yesterday, not with a guy, but with Loris. She told him how that 'date' was.

Erika heard Anthony's sigh.

Was that a sigh of relief?

"I couldn't imagine what you looked like anymore. I seldom see you," said Erika.

What Erika really wanted to say was, *I miss you!*

She didn't say it, as usual.

Anthony replied, "Huh?! You can't imagine anymore what I looked like. Well, the shape of my face is still the same. I am still good-looking!"

They both laughed at that.

Anthony had to end their conversation, even if he didn't want to. There was an important call from his thesis groupmate that he needed to answer.

As Erika put down the phone, she laughed out loud and

then rolled her eyes in disbelief.

"How conceited!"

Erika said it out loud, although no one was around to hear her.

She knew that Anthony was just joking, and Erika didn't really mean that Anthony was conceited. She knew that Anthony was the very opposite of being conceited.

But she couldn't help but laugh!

I really do miss him.

Two days after they talked on the phone, Erika received an email from Anthony. She couldn't deny her excitement; she knew how busy Anthony was because she is busy too. They are both graduating soon.

She was so anxious.

Opening the email felt like a huge task, especially when the internet was so irritatingly slow.

Reading the title «***Thank you and Until Then***» in her inbox was enough to send her to the edge.

She didn't understand why, and she was getting so emotional.

Why is Anthony sending a farewell message so early? And why am I sad?

Subject: Untitled

Untitled

Why will you go away
Wen all you want is to stay
Why will you hold on to memory
When you can write a new story

There are times you want to cry so hard
Because separation hurts so much
But it is really worth it, you should ask
A waste of energy, is that what you want?

There's sadness you can't express or say
Sadness you feel so deep inside everyday
This sorrow feelings flowing within you
Controlling everything you think or do

Your soul is sad, it becomes you
So try to get away from this blue
Think of those who makes you smile
People in your life, worth your while

Sometimes, things do happen
That you don't have control over
No matter how you try to break from it
It never goes away, not even a bit

Just face it, learn from the experience
It will soon be part of your reminiscence
Life is not just about sorrows and laughter
It is more complex and full of wonders

I pray that no matter what happens, although you and I might not be together, may we always be in each other's memories, thoughts, laughter, soul, and heart. And remember that you are always a part of me—a part of my life.

Thank you and Until Then
Just remember…that is all I ask….

Anthony
February 17

After the result of our thesis defense

After reading the poem and the message, Erika has a mixed feeling about it.

In one way, she was glad that Anthony sent it to her after he had just finished with his final oral defense. It only means that he's thinking about her, and he also wanted to share his success with her.

Erika also remembered what Anthony said about poems; he collected them. He doesn't usually give poems to anyone. For him, his poem is his way of expressing his thoughts and feelings.

But she also felt sadness.

Her tears came down so freely, no matter how she tried to control them.

She read the poem many times, trying to dig deeper into the message. She can feel every word. And yes, she wanted Anthony to stay.

Erika is not so convinced that it was really about saying goodbye.

But what else is it then?

It's getting real!

She knew it would happen eventually. They have their own goals in life. They have plans and dreams.

Thank you and Until Then
Just remember…that is all I ask….

Erika kept crying.

She can't help her tears from pouring.

Knowing and being ready are totally different things. She's not ready. She knew she didn't.

Erika tried to compose herself.

When her tears dried up, she began to wonder why the poem doesn't have a title.

Or is 'Untitled' really the title of the poem?

Was it intentional?

She printed the email.

Erika wanted to treasure the poem he wrote. She wanted to carry it with her so she could read it whenever and wherever she is.

She knew that Anthony wrote it wholeheartedly, and she could feel Anthony's emotion in the poem while reading it.

Erika doesn't want Anthony to know that she's starting to have feelings for him.

Is it infatuation? Maybe!

Is this love?

She doesn't know!

He will be leaving anyway.

Although it is not graduation yet, but it feels like he's

already saying goodbye in a way.

That's what's going through her mind.

With a heavy heart, Erika answered the email.

She tried so hard not to express any emotion she was feeling.

She doesn't want Anthony to pick up any hint about her feelings.

Subject: Hello!

Anthony,

Hey. Why are you saying farewell? The poem is well written and very emotional. By the way, how was the defense?

N.B. I printed the poem for safekeeping.

Erika

Based on Anthony's reply, she learned that the defense went well, and that he passed.

He was thankful and touched by what she had done with his poem.

Anthony had told Erika that he was able to finish the poem he wrote in Legazpi during the Youth festival. He just didn't know where he placed it.

He has planned on sending it to her when he finds it; if not, he will just write another poem for her.

A week after she received the "Untitled" poem, she got a text message from Anthony asking if she would be attending the concert.

Anthony was referring to the upcoming concert of the Philippines most popular band at that time, ***The A Band***. The band will be holding a live concert in CU.

It was a once-in-a-lifetime opportunity for her to see them perform live, so she wouldn't miss it!

Erika was sure that Anthony would be at the concert too.

The day came, and the concert was a few hours away.

Erika got a text message from Anthony saying he couldn't come to watch the concert.

> Hey Erika. I'm feeling under the weather right now. As much as I would like to watch the concert, I have to pass. Enjoy and stay safe. See you when I see you.☺

Erika felt the disappointment filter through her.

She was so excited for this concert, knowing she and Anthony could watch it together.

This should be their first concert to attend together. At the same time, she was worried about him.

She replied,

> OK. I hope you get well soon. It's sad that you can't watch the concert, though. ☺

Ding!

Another message from Anthony.

You can tell me about the concert later. ☺

At the concert, Erika couldn't focus.

The crowd was wild and loud. But Erika was not feeling the party vibe.

Although Loris and Juris were with her, she wished Anthony was too.

For Erika, it was not the same without Anthony.

Chapter 3

Ding!

Erika hears the message tone on her mobile phone. Her reminiscing is temporarily interrupted.

She looks at her phone and sees that the message is from Anthony.

"Oh, shit! I forgot to message Anthony." Erika muses while trying to figure out where they are now.

The bus is traveling through Ayala Avenue now.

OMG!

She will soon be in Buendia.

Hei. Where are you now? Did you forget to send me a message or is it traffic? ☺

Erika fumbles with her mobile phone as she hurries with her reply.

Yes, I forgot. Sorry. I am now on Ayala Ave.

Erika shakes her head in disbelief. She was so immersed in her memory that she forgot to send a message.

It was a little over twelve o'clock when Erika got out of the bus at Buendia.

Since it is summer and in the middle of the day, the sun is strikingly hot. Many people are hurrying in different directions. Erika can hear the incoming and outgoing trains from the LRT station right above where she is standing.

On the side of the road, there are many sidewalk vendors selling almost everything one can think of, like food, drinks, cigarettes, fancy jewelries, and bags, among others.

Erika looks at the small Donut stall on the far end of the corner, and she feels hungry. She suddenly craves for donuts. It has been many hours since she had her breakfast.

"It has been ages since I ate a strawberry-filled donut!" whispers Erika while walking towards the stall. But before she even gets there, she has a second thought.

Maybe I'll just wait until I meet Anthony, so we can decide together where we can eat lunch.

Erika rolls her eyes. She can't believe she's been talking to herself while walking on a busy street in Buendia.

Erika sighs!

She tries to remember where exactly they will meet. Anthony said that they would meet at Buendia Terminal.

Maybe I messed up by sending a late text message. Anthony is probably on his way – just late.

Erika hears the sound of an incoming call, and at the same time, she can feel her phone vibrating in her sling bag. She takes out her phone from the bag to take the call. She knows it's from Anthony based on the ringtone.

"Hello," says Erika.

"Hey. Where are you now?" Anthony asks.

It is so noisy that Erika has difficulty hearing what Anthony is saying. She asks if he could repeat what he just said, but this time louder.

Anthony repeats as Erika wished.

Erika is standing near the Donut stall so as not to be bumped by people passing by. At the same time, Erika is being careful.

"I am standing near the Donut stall, not far from the bus terminal." Erika says.

"Ok. I can see you now," replies Anthony.

As Erika hears what Anthony just said, she presses the end button on her phone without saying goodbye.

She looks around, trying to see where Anthony is.

If he can see where I am, it only means that he's not far from here.

And there he is!

Standing tall on the other side of the road, looking directly at her. He's smiling brightly.

"I miss that smile." Erika whispers.

One look at him, even from a distance, is enough for her heart to go wild. It is wreaking havoc on her peace of mind, and it is getting beyond her control. The feeling that she thought she had buried a long time ago is very much alive right now.

Anthony waits before he crosses the street, making sure that it is safe. All the while, Erika is just staring at him.

She can't believe that she is seeing him again. It has been years since Erika last saw Anthony. But it feels like it was just yesterday, at their graduation ceremony.

She can vividly recall that evening, as if it happened last night and not four years ago.

:

:

:

:
Manalo, Erika B.

Erika heard the assistant secretary general announce her name. She walked to the stage to get her diploma. In her mind, while doing so, Erika dedicated her diploma to her mother.

The university president, together with the secretary general, department deans, and registrar, were all standing up on the stage to shake hands with each and every graduate.

On her way down to where she was sitting, she saw Anthony smiling while clapping his hands. She waved her hands to Anthony, and he, in return, made a thumbs up sign. And all the while, Erika was thinking that it was her biggest achievement so far, and she was thankful that she had done it.

After the ceremony, Anthony came to her and congratulated her.

"Finally! Congratulations to both of us!"

And for the first time, Anthony hugged Erika.

"Yes! Congrats! Wow, with a special award! Magna cum laude and best in thesis! You're the man!" Erika said.

She smiled at Anthony.

She was really proud of his achievement, and she knew that he deserved it. Anthony worked so hard.

Erika was so impressed with how Anthony was able to balance everything, given all the extra activities he had. And with flying colors!

Impressive!

Anthony said, "Thank you! Just so you know, you are

my inspiration!"

He winked and smiled at her.

Erika smiled shyly and didn't know what to say. She just gave Anthony her graduation gift to him instead.

"Oh, thank you. I forgot my gift to you. It was in my room, and I forgot to bring it with me. I really am sorry." With a red face, Anthony said.

"No problem. It's no big deal. Don't beat yourself about it." Erika replied.

They didn't have much time to talk since both their families were waiting for them.

"OK. See you when I see you!"

Anthony will be returning to Legazpi the very next day together with his family.

And that was the last time Erika saw Anthony.

Two days after the graduation ceremony, Erika went back to the campus for the final meeting of the student council.

They also need to clean their office for the next set of officers. After that, all the council officers gathered under the Evita stage, facing the big green football field of CU. She then saw Juris.

Juris is Anthony's first cousin on his mother side of the family. Anthony's mother is an older sister to Juris' mom. While Anthony was studying at CU, he lived with Juris' family. They were, in fact, like brothers. They were very close to each other, although Juris is one year younger. Juris was a lot taller than Anthony and very athletic. He was a varsity player at CU.

Juris was walking towards her with a gift in his hand, accompanied by a card.

He gave them to Erika.

"Hi. Congratulations, Erika!" greeted Juris.

Erika remembered that Anthony forgot to bring this gift with him on graduation day. She understood why. They were all busy at that time. It was an eventful day, with all the rush and hustle of graduation.

"Hello, Juris! How are you?" was her reply.

"I'm good. Here's your graduation gift from Anthony," said Juris.

"He was so busy that day, especially after his family arrived. It was very chaotic at home; that's why he forgot to bring that gift. He then asked me before they traveled back to Legazpi if I could give it to you." Juris continued.

"Thank you," Erika said while accepting the gift and the card. She didn't open the gift. She would wait until she's home.

"And, by the way, can I say something?" Juris asked her, seemingly shy.

"Yes, what is it?" asked Erika.

"Anthony told me he wanted to stay a little longer that night, after graduation. He wanted to spend more time with you. He had no choice, though. His family couldn't wait because they already had arranged a celebration back at Legazpi." Said Juris.

"What can I say?" murmured Erika.

She controlled herself not to cry. She missed Anthony more and more as she heard Juris talk about him.

"Anthony is very fond of you and always talks about you. And personally, I think you look better together. Both of you seem happier when together." Juris continued.

"We are friends. Of course, we are fond of each other!" said Erika.

Anthony was the closest friend she had from the male kingdom.

She tried to sound okay. She didn't want to make it more obvious to Juris about what she was feeling for Anthony. Erika was not comfortable with her feelings being known.

The only person who knows about her feelings for Anthony is Loris, her best friend.

Juris smiled and stared at her knowingly.

He then said, "I understand. Both of you, I think, are in denial. Anthony told me the same thing when I brought it up. I just want both of you to be happy. I wish you and Anthony a happy ending, you know." Explained Juris.

"I am not in denial. I just don't know or can't explain what I truly feel." Erika defended herself.

"You miss him, right? And in your moment of solitude, have you ever wondered why you seemed different when you were with him? How does Anthony act when he is with you? It was like you and Anthony were in a special bubble when in each other's company. It's like a different world where only you and Anthony exist, and all the others don't." Juris explained.

"I didn't know. Are we?" Erika asked.

Do we really have this bubble around us from when we were together?

"I teased Anthony about it. He said the same thing. But really, you and he can talk with each other without saying a word. Both of you look at each other, and you understand one another. It's crazy sometimes! The connection between you two is there! I sometimes can't comprehend at all," said Juris, shaking his head.

Erika just stared at him. She was in disbelief at what he said.

Really?

Are we like that together?

They talked about me!

"OK. I think I have said too much already," said Juris while scratching his head.

"If Anthony learned, I said that he was for sure going to kill me!" said Juris, and then laughed out loud.

Juris was with friends and co-varsity players, and they were waiting for him, so they didn't have much time to talk anymore.

He just waved and said, "Take care, Erika. Until next time."

"Thank you, Juris, and give my regards to your mom!" Erika replied and waved her hands, too.

"Will do! And, Erika, can you please say hello to Loris from me?" Juris pleaded.

"I knew it!" Erika gladly replied.

"Knew what?"

Juris was suddenly confused.

"You had a thing for Loris, isn't it?" Erika teased.

"Yes!" Juris' simple reply.

"I was just kidding! But really?"

Erika was shocked when Juris admitted that he had a 'thing' for Loris. She was just kidding about it.

Juris just smiled at her and winked before he continued walking towards a group of basketball players waiting for him.

If only I could be like Juris.

Erika ignored the look the other council members were giving her.

A look of curiosity.

Erika opened the card after Juris left.

It was a 3D card that Erika saw and admired on the internet when she was looking for something she could give to Loris and Anthony.

The overall background color was her favorite pink, with a lady popping on top wearing a traditional black graduation gown and cap.

Erika thought that the design of the card was beautiful.

Erika read the written message inside.

Dear Erika,

Congratulations! We did it!

I hope all your dreams will come true. This is just the beginning. We don't know where fate will take us. Whatever happens, let us not forget what we have built between us.

See you when I see you. ☺ I will miss you!

Oremus Pro Invicem!

Anthony

Erika stared at the card.

She felt motionless for a while.

There was a sudden emotion that filtered through her heart after reading Anthony's message.

Erika doesn't know why she felt like she wanted to cry again.

She tried to control her emotions because she didn't want to explain to other council officers why she was crying.

But at least he will miss me.

"He doesn't know how much I miss him right this moment." Erika whispered.

The emotion was new to her. She hadn't felt it before; that was why she had trouble dealing with it.

Oremus Pro Invicem!

What does it mean?

She didn't know whom to ask. She didn't even know what language it was. The problem was that if Erika asked someone, she might have to explain where she got it. And Erika doesn't want that.

Chapter 4

It may all have started with a simple introduction, jokes and laughter, a piece of paper, a hi and hello every now and then, and exchanging messages using text or email, but those are enough for Erika's feeling for Anthony to grow a hundredfold.

Although she and Anthony haven't seen each other for a long time, her feelings for him are still there. It is as if nothing has changed. And now she's looking at him again, four years after that last time.

How would I react?

How would I behave?

I hope I will not stammer, whispers Erika.

It is not the same as exchanging messages through texts or emails and conversing face-to-face after not doing so for a long time. The distance sometimes makes it awkward.

I don't want to mess up, muses Erika.

Oh, please, not today!

She hopes her feelings for him are not that obvious. Erika remembers her conversation with Loris.

"I wondered where Anthony is right now and what he's doing," said Erika to Loris.

They were eating at the popular local fast-food restaurant that offers Erika's favorite, crispy chicken and spaghetti. It was two weeks after their graduation.

"You miss him," said Loris to Erika.

It was not a question but an affirmation.

"I know you have feelings for him, Erika. Don't even try to deny it." Loris continued.

Loris has been Erika's friend since day one of their college lives. Loris knew her very well.

"I know. I won't deny it. You know me. My face is very expressive, to the point that it's annoying me already."

"I know it, girl! You always brighten up when someone mentions Anthony's name. Your eyes even sparkle when he's around." Loris said this while smiling.

"OMG! Am I that obvious? I think Juris said something like that, too, when he handed me the gift from Anthony. I hope Anthony doesn't know."

Erika exclaimed while blushing.

"Oh, I'm not sure about that. Maybe he knew, or maybe he didn't. But here's the thing: I think he has feelings for you, too." Loris grinned at Erika.

"Have you asked Juris about Anthony and me? Why did you say something that I already heard from Juris?" She accused Loris, and Erika glared at her best friend.

Erika continued, "And how can you say that Anthony has any feelings for me? He never showed any indication that he had feelings for me. He used to joke around with me; you know him. And besides, how can Anthony be interested in me when there are a lot of girls on the campus that have a crush on him?" Erika was almost out of breath when she finished.

"Aren't you one of those girls?" Loris jokingly said to her.

"And to answer your questions, I haven't talked to Juris about you and Anthony, and I am not blind, so I can see how you and Anthony behave when in each other's company."

Erika blushed because Loris was right.

She had a crush on Anthony. Only her best friend, Loris, knew about it. Erika wouldn't be able to live another day if Anthony would ever find that out.

"Anthony is serious all the time. I think his jokes are always just for you. And my guess is that joking with you is Anthony's form of tenderness towards you, so he can express his feelings for you in a very subtle way." Loris litany to her.

Erika thought it was impossible that Anthony had the same feelings for her as she had for him.

"Hi! It's good to see you again, Erika," says Anthony. Hearing Anthony's voice stops Erika from continuing her 'down memory lane' moment. Anthony then hugs her.

"Hello. It's good to see you, too!"

It was a bit of a shock to her when Anthony greeted her with a hug. Not that she's complaining now!

They had never greeted each other with a hug before. The only time they hugged was when they congratulated each other on graduation day.

"You are blooming, and somehow you looked different," says Anthony while staring at her.

He seems to study her face, which makes her so anxious and conscious.

Erika can't blame Anthony for noticing the changes in her. After all, Erika gains weight, and she has a lighter skin complexion now than before. Erika also had her dental braces removed. All of these make wonders for her facial structure, she guesses.

And her hair!

Erika has recently been to a hair salon for a cellophane

treatment. This was a semi-permanent treatment to add some luster and shine to her long, wavy hair. She chose a color not far from her hair's natural color, the darkest of brown.

She can't explain the blooming part, though. She doesn't even know she's blooming until Anthony mentions that.

Maybe seeing him made her blush, which gave her a blooming effect?

Who knows?!

Anthony is wearing very light-colored Khaki pants, a plain white polo shirt with just a check symbol on the upper left side, and very stylish white canvas sneaker shoes.

He looks so clean and fresh in white.

How can he look so fresh in the scourging heat of the day?

He doesn't look to be sweating at all. On the other hand, she feels like she needs another shower.

Erika went for comfort when she chose her outfit today. She is wearing her favorite stretch jeans, a light-yellow blouse with different print designs, and her favorite women's hook & loop fastener backless mesh sneakers in white color, too.

On weekdays, she normally wears her work uniform. She has a work uniform, both the pants and blouse and the skirt and blouse combination, with black formal shoes to match.

On weekends, when going to TLS, since they don't have a uniform there, she wears pants, a t-shirt, and rubber shoes.

Erika is thinking now that she should have suggested meeting him in Alabang rather than in Manila.

Alabang is the middle point between Laguna and

Manila. Erika could have spared travel time and much sweat.

"Hey! Penny for your thoughts!" Anthony says.

There's a smile on his face, as if he could read her thoughts. She blushes and feels the warmth on her face.

"Are you hungry? Shall we eat first before we go to *The Mall Place*? Or do you want to eat when we get there?" Anthony asks her.

She's hungry, but she doesn't want to waste much time now.

"We can eat lunch at The Mall Place. But do you mind if I buy a strawberry-filled donut before we go?"

Anthony smiles at Erika and then buys her donuts.

She insists on paying for them herself, but Anthony is not taking them. Knowing full well that it will just be a lost battle for her, she gives up and lets Anthony pay for the donuts.

They take LRT going to The Mall Place, which is located in Pedro Gil, Manila. They walk from the LRT station to the mall. Anthony holds her hand as they walk together. Erika can't explain what she is feeling at that very moment. She likes it anyway.

On the back of her mind, while they are walking, she is singing the song of Yeng Constantino, "Hawak-kamay", which simply means *holding hands*.

Erika wants the song to be Anthony's promise of being with her as they journey through the world of emptiness and uncertainty.

She wishes that Anthony's gesture of holding her hand is like a promise not to leave her on this journey alone.

I will be more than happy.

I will be ecstatic!

She is smiling from ear to ear, and she can't help it.

Inside the mall, they go first to the cinema section to check the schedule for Spiderman and The Scorpion King movies. Those two are the most popular movies right now.

Anthony has already seen Spiderman, but since Erika hasn't, and the movie has a two o'clock time slot for the guaranteed seats, they decide that it is the one they are going to watch.

The cinema section is full of moviegoers, so they are hoping that it will be worth it when two o'clock comes. They still have a little over an hour to eat.

Erika and Anthony go to the first restaurant they see inside the mall. Upon entering the restaurant, Anthony directs Erika to a table located on the right corner near the counter. When they are already seated, Erika orders baked macaroni pasta with garlic bread and a glass of orange juice, while Anthony orders a pizza and a glass of cola.

As they eat, Anthony asks Erika, "So, tell me, what kept you busy all this time?"

"Well, where to start?" Erika answers.

"From the beginning, perhaps?" Anthony replies in a jokeful manner.

"I think I have this gray area in my mind about where the beginning actually is." Erika smirks.

Anthony laughs. At the same time, he waits for her to continue.

Erika wonders why she's almost lost for words. She doesn't usually like this. She is, in fact, a very loquacious person if given a different circumstance.

But right now, in front of Anthony, she can't find her

wit or her loquaciousness.

She's looking at Anthony but not really seeing him.

She's freaking out!

That is the only explanation she can think of!

And then it happens.

When Erika opens her mouth to answer Anthony, she speaks non-stop. Almost as if she's not pausing.

"As I told you on the phone last time, I am working in one of the automotive industries in Santa Rosa Laguna as their financial analyst. I commute every day from home to Crossing terminal in Calamba. And from the terminal, there is a shuttle bus provided by our company for all the employees within the area, which I take to lessen the hustle of traveling to and from work. It also saves me money. Then, a year later, I learned from a friend that The Law School (TLS) in Taft Avenue is offering an executive class for working professionals like me. So, without thinking clearly, I just grabbed the opportunity. I went to TLS and fulfilled all their requirements, and voila, here I am, enrolled in law school! I have been busy ever since."

OMG!

Did I really say all that so fast and without a pause?

Erika wants to roll her eyes. In fact, in her mind, Erika is already kicking herself for babbling.

I feel and act like a dork!

Ok. Deep breath, Erika. You are usually articulate and very loquacious. You just have to make sure that your mouth is totally in sync with your head right now before you open your mouth again to speak.

Stop babbling, for heaven's sake, Erika!

These are the thoughts going on inside her head right

now.

Anthony grins, as if trying to figure out what is wrong with her, and Erika can't blame him.

She is acting weird.

"I am so proud of you, to be honest!"

Erika hears Anthony reply to her babbling episode.

Erika didn't want to make any comment on what she had just heard from Anthony. She is afraid that she will stammer and embarrass herself again if she opens her mouth.

"You are chasing your dream, Erika. I hope one day I can, too," says Anthony.

He then continues and asks, "By the way, how was your first year in law school? Was it difficult?"

Before Erika can answer, their lunch arrives. At the same time, Anthony's phone rings, and he excuses himself for a while to answer it.

When Anthony returns to the table, they start to eat.

They have very little time to continue their chat. They need to finish lunch quickly and go upstairs to the cinema section to buy tickets.

It will be a long queue, so they need to hurry.

The cinema is already so full, but luckily, they have guaranteed seats.

To protect her from all the people going in and out of the cinema, Anthony puts his hand on Erika's shoulder and uses his body as a shield as they go to their place.

Erika can't concentrate on the movie.

They are seating so close to each other that she can almost hear Anthony's breathing and feels his every movement.

This is so insane.

They are quiet the whole time.

She's busier assessing her feelings at that moment than really watching the film.

Thinking of them being together is a lot better than watching the scenes on the big screen.

The Dolby sound might be loud, but her heartbeats are louder.

When the movie ends, Anthony asks her what she thinks about the movie.

Erika doesn't want to tell Anthony that she didn't really watch, so she says instead that the movie is "OK!"

Anthony stares at her, and he seems not so convinced of her "OK" answer. He didn't call her on it, though.

Chapter 5

Anthony wants to buy a new mobile phone, so they go to the ground floor of the mall. He holds Erika's hand again while they walk. Erika can't help but feel like they are boyfriend and girlfriend.

Do friends hold hands while walking inside the mall?

Well, Anthony is acting like her boyfriend in her defense, and she's not complaining.

Not at all!

Erika grins with the thought.

After Anthony bought his phone, they go around the mall, trying to find the foreign exchange (forex) area. He says that he has with him some US dollars that he needs to change to pesos. There is a long line of people in the forex area; therefore, Anthony decides not to change his dollars anymore.

As they walk away from the line of people, they turn left. They continue walking until they reach the opposite side of the mall. They see *The Kids Side* area.

'The Kids Side' is a beautiful place for children to have fun while inside the mall. Although they don't have any kids with them, Erika and Anthony enter the area and sit on the vacant bench they see near the slides. Erika notices that most of the people inside *The Kids Side* are families. There is music, too, but for Erika, the volume is too loud for her to have a decent conversation with Anthony.

Erika shakes her head, annoyed at herself for thinking

that way.

Just enjoy, Erika. Relax!

"Haven't you noticed something?" Anthony asks.

"What? Was it the music being too loud or the fact that we are the only ones here without a kid to accompany?" Erika replies.

Anthony smiles—the smile that always captures Erika's heart.

"Yes, that too! But haven't you noticed that they are playing the same song over and over?" He asks.

Anthony looks at Erika. He then gestures for her to listen to the song. Erika sits still for a while and listens to the music. She smiles as she recognizes the song.

"Do you know the song?" Anthony asks.

"Yes! In fact, I am!" Erika exclaims.

Her eyes are suddenly bright with excitement. She can't help herself but sing along with it. Anthony just looks and listens as Erika sings along with the song joyfully.

After Erika's sing-along session, Anthony gets up and walks toward one of the kids' rides. He then says to Erika that he wants to try it, but there's a height limit for the ride.

Anthony then says jokingly, "Next time, we can bring a kid with us."

OK. So, there will be a 'next time' for us.

Wait, what?

Kid?

Did Anthony say we can bring a 'kid' next time?

Erika smiles and says, "We'll see!"

They stay in that place for an hour.

"Maybe we can drink coffee or have a light snack,

perhaps," says Anthony.

They are now strolling inside the mall. He then looks at his wristwatch to check the time.

"Yeah. I better drink and have something to eat before I travel back to Laguna." Erika replies.

She is a little hungry, but Erika doesn't want a full meal. She was not able to eat all the lunch she ordered earlier. Erika's emotion was getting the better of her, and it affected her appetite. So, coffee and bread, or perhaps cake, are okay.

Anthony and Erika walk towards the famous coffee shop. They saw that coffee shop earlier while strolling around looking for the foreign exchange area.

Luckily for them, they find a place to sit inside the coffee shop. Anthony asks her what she wants. Erika tells him she wants an ice-cold Frappuccino and a slice of chocolate cake.

Anthony goes to the counter to place an order. He comes back with her order and a hot cup of black coffee for him. He, too, has a slice of the same chocolate cake as hers.

Erika feels relaxed as she sits opposite Anthony, sipping coffee. Anthony asks the same question he asked her earlier, when they were waiting for their lunch, about her first year in law school.

She answers him enthusiastically.

"It was tough! I had five subjects compressed into two days, Saturday and Sunday. All these subjects demand so much of my time. So, after every workday, when I am at home, I stay awake up to two o'clock in the morning, just to memorize all the laws. We had court cases to read and analyze every week, too. That's why I have been reading a lot of cases from SCRA," explains Erika.

Erika can still feel it in her bones—the tiredness she got after a year in law school. Erika almost gave up her dream after her health was compromised because of stress.

All those sleepless nights and stress are catching up to her.

She memorized the codes verbatim. This means including the commas, hyphens, and periods. Her favorite code, and the one she can't forget, is Article 3 of the Civil Code of the Philippines.

Not only that, her first class always begins at seven in the morning, and her last class ends at six in the evening. She traveled back and forth to Laguna and Manila. She's usually on the bus at around five in the morning. She ate her breakfast, usually a sandwich that her mother prepared for her, on the bus while reading more of the codes.

"What is SCRA?" Anthony asks.

Erika sips her coffee before she replies, "Supreme Court Report Annotated. It was really tough, especially when I had overtime at work. I was exhausted almost every day. In between breaks at work, I was reading and memorizing laws. I always bring with me wherever I go the book *The Revised Penal Code of the Philippines*."

"I can't imagine all the things you've gone through. But, in fairness, you are blooming. The stress suits you, perhaps," says Anthony while he stares at Erika.

Erika laughs.

When she calms down, she answers, "It's funny that you say that! I think I eat more when I am stressed. Thus, I gained weight instead of losing it."

"My ortho even said before that she had never encountered a patient that eats a lot with braces on."

Anthony laughs at that, too.

"That's why you looked different. You had dental braces before," says Anthony.

Erika blushes.

She didn't intend on telling Anthony about her dental braces. The words were already out of her mouth before she could stop herself from saying them.

Anthony looks at her and sees her discomfort. He then changes the topic back to law school.

"What are the usual subjects during the first year of law school? You said you had five. What are they?" inquires Anthony.

"Well, I had Criminal law, Persons and Family Relations, Constitutional law, Legal Writing, and Legal Research,"

She says that all her professors were using an autocratic method of teaching, especially her lady professor in Persons and Family Relations.

"Every time I was in her class, I was nervous. I was always praying that she wouldn't call my name for recitation. My professor used to call someone to stand in the class and usually asked them to recite codes for an hour or more. VER-BA-TIM!"

Anthony listens to her as she explains.

"What about you? What have you been doing all this time?" asks Erika.

She wants to know why he seldom sent messages after they graduated. Yes, he sent a few, but Erika misses those times when he's always sending an email or a simple text message to her.

"I was busy too. After we graduated, I went back to Legazpi to be with my family. I worked there for less than a year. At the same time, I was sending work applications in Manila. I decided to take up a master's degree in philosophy while working. Luckily, I got a job offer from the company I am with right now. That gave me the opportunity to pursue my master's degree and work at the same time," replies Anthony.

"Why philosophy, and why in Manila?" asks Erika.

"I wanted to experience the Manila life. It was one of my dreams to study at a university within Metro Manila. As to why philosophy? Well, right after graduation, when I was sitting outside our house overlooking Mt. Mayon, I thought of you. I can vividly see you in my mind. Your fascination with the law mesmerized me! It clicked to me that I also wanted to be a lawyer, but first I have to finish my master's degree, as I promised my father I would. So, I thought that if I take a master's degree in philosophy, this will eventually help fulfill my promise to my dad, realize my dream of studying in Manila, and prepare me for law school in the future," explains Anthony.

"So, all these questions about law school, are you just curious—or do you want some inside knowledge?" Erika teases.

"I already have basic knowledge. I just want to hear from you about your own personal experience and what you think of it now that you are already in law school. I am always fascinated to hear your enthusiasm about it. Erika, you always light up every time you talk about law and law school. I noticed that when we were in the university," answers Anthony.

Am I?

Erika is trying to remember the time we talked about law school.

Too many to count!

"And, before I forget, the reason I asked you to go out with me today was because of this," Anthony says, giving Erika a white envelope he took in his pocket.

He then continues, "I want to give it to you personally."

The envelope is not that big. It looks like an invitation.

"What's that?" Erika asks.

"It's for you. You can open it," Anthony encourages Erika. He smiles, which makes Erika jitter.

She takes the envelope from Anthony. All the while, her mind is trying to calm her heart. She is nervous, and she can feel her heart beating so fast. At the same time, her temperature rises.

Relax, Erika!

It's just an envelope. Just open it to find out what it really is about!

Erika opens the envelope slowly. It is an invitation to Anthony's graduation.

"Next week?" Erika speaks her thoughts aloud.

"Yeah. Why? Is there a problem?" asks Anthony.

There's a hint of worry in his voice. He can see the expression on Erika's face.

"No, nothing. Is it okay if I bring Loris with me to your graduation? I'm sure it will be late before I can get home," says Erika.

She stares at the invitation while trying to figure out

what *Oremus Pro Invicem* means. He wrote the same phrase on the card she received after their graduation.

"Sure. No problem," replies Anthony.

"What is Oremus Pro Invicem?" She can't keep her curiosity anymore, so she asks.

Before Anthony can reply to her question, Erika continues with, "You wrote the same thing on the card last time. Until now, I haven't found out what that phrase means."

"I was actually hoping that you would send me a message about that last time," replies Anthony.

He then smiles at Erika.

"But at the same time, I also expect that you wouldn't. You are usually stubborn to ask." He continues.

Erika listens to Anthony speak, and not saying a word. She feels her cheeks warm up.

"Well, it's a Latin word, which means *let us pray for each other.*" Anthony stares at Erika while he explains.

Erika straightens her sitting position. She then fixes the hair that keeps falling on her face. Anthony follows Erika's every move. He looks at her right arm, and the smile on his face gets wider.

"Do you like that bracelet? It looks good on you." Anthony asks Erika.

He is referring to the bracelet Erika is wearing. It is the bracelet she got from Anthony as a graduation gift.

Erika recalls that she opened the gift immediately when she got home that day. She was in awe as she saw what was inside.

She likes it very much. She's been wearing this all the time, except when taking a shower and sleeping.

"Yes, I like it. Thank you. You know well what I like." Erika answers.

The bracelet is a silver one with a red heart and pink flower charm.

"Of course I do. I know you, Erika." Anthony's simple reply.

But the way Anthony is looking at Erika right now is telling her that he's not only referring to bracelets.

In between sipping their coffees and eating their cakes, they reminisce about their college days. Erika and Anthony talk about work, too. They laugh a lot in between stories.

They miss each other; Erika is sure of that. Although no one of them says it verbally, she knows they miss the times they were together.

Erika looks at the big wall clock inside the coffee shop and is shocked to see that it is already half past seven o'clock. She needs to be in Buendia if she wants to take the eight o'clock schedule of the bus going to Laguna.

"I need to be going now. It will be late again before I'll be home," says Erika worriedly.

Anthony looks at his wristwatch and then nods at her.

Erika notices that Anthony is still wearing the watch he's been using since college days. It gives Erika an idea of what she will give as a graduation gift to Anthony.

"I'm sorry that we have to meet here in Manila. My schedule is so full of all my work and the graduation rush." Anthony says.

There is a hint of seriousness in his voice and expression.

"It's OK, I do understand." Erika timidly replies.

"I am used to traveling back and forth here anyway."

"I'll take you to the bus terminal, then I will go straight to the campus. I have a meeting for the upcoming graduation. I hope to visit you one day in Laguna." Anthony says to her.

Erika and Anthony walk out of the coffee shop using the other door. This leads them directly outside of the mall. Anthony takes Erika's hand, and together they walk towards Pedro Gil LRT station.

They come to the bus terminal with seven minutes to spare.

Before going on the bus, Erika turns to Anthony and gives him an envelope, and then she smiles at him. Erika asks him not to open it yet.

Anthony says nothing. He only stares at her.

Anthony hugs Erika. This time, Erika hugs him back.

Erika goes inside the bus and finds a seat beside the window. She looks down and waves to Anthony as the bus starts moving. When she can't see Anthony any longer, she lets out a sigh.

She has these mixed feelings after spending time with Anthony. She becomes more confused than ever before.

They didn't say goodbye to each other again.

I guess we both don't want to say goodbye; this is what lingers in Erika's mind.

She felt Anthony's emotions in that hug.

Is it possible that he felt it too?

Ding!

Erika hears the sound of the incoming text message; she has this hunch that the text is from Anthony.

"I hope he didn't open the envelope yet." Erika whispers as she tries to find her mobile phone in the bag.

Hey. Safe travels. Please send me a
message when you get home. ☺

Erika smiles after reading the message and then types a reply.

Hey. That was fast! Thank you,
and I will. Safe travels, too!

She relaxes into her seat.

It will be a long trip, but she's used to it as she travels back and forth to Manila every weekend.

Erika replays what has happened over and over in her mind. She tries to assess her feelings. There is no denying that the feelings she had for Anthony are still there. She worries about his reaction when he finally opens the envelope she gave him.

Ding!

Another message arrives, and this time it is from Loris.

Hi sis! Are you still with Anthony?

She smiles and replies to her best friend, saying she is now on the bus going home.

Not long after she sent her reply, Erika receives another message from Loris telling her that Loris will be coming over to her tomorrow because Loris can't wait to hear from her what happened to her 'date' with Anthony.

Erika just rolls her eyes and does not bother replying.

Chapter 6

Anthony is in his room inside the apartment he's renting in Quezon City. He works in the Human Resources Department at the Telecommunication Company on Commonwealth Avenue in the same city.

After he accompanied Erika to the bus station earlier, he went straight to the university for a late meeting and a graduation rehearsal.

He had a very long day.

It was a very tiring, but fulfilling and happy day for him.

He's used to being so tired, as he usually juggles between his work and his master studies.

But being this happy is something he's not used to—not for a very long while, anyway.

Seeing and talking to Erika again after four years of not doing so is very overwhelming. He loves every second of it. There is also this special feeling that he can't describe every time he is with Erika.

Anthony stares at the envelope he's holding.

He doesn't really know what to expect.

A letter, perhaps?

Ever since they became friends, Anthony can't recall a single time when Erika gave him a written letter. Their communication was mostly through phone calls, text messages, and emails.

So, Anthony was surprised when Erika gave him an envelope that looked like there's a letter inside right before she went inside the bus.

Anthony wanted to open it right there and then, but Erika asked him not to open it yet. So, he controlled himself.

Staring at the envelope, he is trying to assess the emotion he is currently having.

Anthony opens the envelop. To his surprise, there is no letter inside; instead, there is a handwritten poem on a piece of stationary paper.

"Who still uses stationary paper these days?" Anthony whispers, a bright smile on his face.

That's what he likes about Erika. She does what she wants.

Her handwriting is very legible, elegant, and sexy, Anthony thinks.

"I didn't know Erika wrote poems."

He smiles again.

He's been smiling ever since he saw Erika today. And he keeps smiling even after.

Anthony is liking what he's feeling.

Someone asked me

Someone asked me, What's my story?
I paused briefly and thought about it
I dug a little deeper in my memory
Should I tell him about you and me?

I don't know where to start
Maybe from the beginning isn't bad
Recalling that day was just ordinary
Though it's not summer, it's a little sunny

I can always picture it in my mind
Smile so bright that it made me blind
And as the days and years went by
Feelings became clearer than the sky

Ups and downs and spinning around
Making me dizzy, wanting the ground
It's becoming like a roller coaster ride
I have to hold on and enjoy it to survive

I wonder how many twilights will pass
Before the story of you and me subsides
As more chapters start to unfold
I hope I can remember it as I get old

I have to let it be part of my story
Write it down and preserve the memory
One day the world will know, maybe
Our very own, the story of you and me

Anthony reads the poem a couple of times more.

There's a lot going on in his mind right now. Anthony is feeling a lot of different emotions that he's trying to control, and he's been controlling all those emotions for a very long time already.

Erika gave him no hint that she writes poems.

How long has she been writing?

And speaking of poems, when will I send my poem to Erika?

Anthony sighs.

He still doesn't know when he will have the courage to give the poem to Erika, as he promised her.

"She is so special to me," whispers Anthony.

He worries that if he gives the poem to Erika, it can change their friendship forever. But he's been keeping the poem for years and he hasn't fulfilled his promise.

Erika is so precious to me that I don't want to lose her.

Anthony stands up from sitting on the bed. He goes to the right corner of his room to get a notebook from the cabinet. He then goes back to where he was sitting earlier.

He opens the notebook and flips through the pages. He doesn't stop until he finds what he's looking for.

Anthony smiles when he finds the poem in the middle of the notebook. This is the exact poem he promised to send Erika a long time ago.

He reads the poem.

After reading, Anthony has decided to send it to Erika.

A thought creeps into his mind. He doesn't know much about her now.

Is there someone special in her life?

He didn't ask Erika about her love life. She didn't ask him either. Their conversation earlier, when they were eating, circled around law school, work, and graduation. They reminisced about their past, too, but never talked about their *relationship status*.

Anthony has been with someone these past years until their relationship ended six months ago.

But Erika is Erika.

She is, and will always be, special to me.

Anthony wonders now if Erika has been or is still in a relationship with someone else, too.

But even just thinking about the possibility irritates Anthony so much.

He doesn't like it at all!

Chapter 7

The calmness of the sea
And the serenity of the sky
Are giving no clues about
The storm in a fragile heart

There is a knock on her bedroom door, as Erika is still lying on her bed. She came home late last night. It was a little almost twelve midnight when she finally reached home. There was heavy traffic on the South Luzon Expressway as usual during the summer season. In addition, there's an ongoing road widening construction along the Alabang road all the way to the Calamba area.

Erika doesn't want to get up early because it is not often that she can stay late in bed.

And it's Sunday, for heaven's sake!

"Erika! Loris is here!"

Erika hears what her mother says on the other side of the door. But she is still sleepy, and she really doesn't want to get up yet.

Her mother knocks again on the door, this time a bit louder and heavier.

"OK, Mom. Can you please tell her to wait a minute or two, please?" Erika replies and begs her mother.

There's no point in ignoring her mother. Erika knows how stubborn her mother is. After all, Erika got her stubbornness from her.

Loris told her last night, as Erika remembers now, that she's coming over to nag at her.

Erika gets up and changes into decent clothes. She also combs her hair before opening her bedroom door.

Since their house is not that big, she sees Loris in the living room, sitting on the sofa right away.

"Good morning," greets Erika to Loris.

"Good day, you mean!" Loris smirks and rolls her eyes at Erika.

"Whatever!" says Erika smirking too.

Erika and Loris have been doing that with each other ever since. They usually smirk at each other when they both have a chance and roll their eyes as often as they can. This makes them laugh every single time.

Just like right now.

It is almost one o'clock in the afternoon.

"It feels like morning to me. Can you give me another couple of minutes to complete my morning routine?" Erika asks.

She then proceeds to the bathroom without waiting for a reply from Loris.

"So, tell me about your date. I want details!" Loris says it with too much excitement.

Loris and Erika are now sitting on the terrace. This was after Erika finished with her routine and ate "brunch." Erika wants to sit on the bench in the garden, but the sun is strikingly hot, so she decides to just stay on the terrace.

Erika's mother serves light snacks for Loris: a sandwich, cashew tarts, and a glass of cold orange juice. Erika is drinking hot green tea, a routine for her every time she finishes eating.

In between eating the bread and sipping juice, Loris keeps asking questions.

"It is not a date, Loris! How many times do I need to

tell you that IT.WAS.NOT.A.DATE?" Erika says with clear emphasis.

Erika keeps telling Loris that she and Anthony did not date. They just went out to catch up with one another. But Loris is not convinced at all.

Well, Erika is not sure anyway if she is trying to convince her best friend Loris or herself.

"It is a date!" says Loris.

She then rolls her eyes at Erika.

"But, anyway, please do tell! I am dying of excitement here. Don't keep me waiting for too long, please!" Loris puts her palms together like in a praying position and pleads with Erika to tell her.

Erika rolls her eyes, too. And they both laugh again.

"OK. I will tell you, but in one condition," says Erika.

"What condition?" asks Loris doubtfully.

"You will stop calling it a date!" says Erika.

Loris says, "Yes," but she crosses her fingers because 'it is a date!'

She knows that she can't get away with this, not with Loris. So Erika tells Loris what happened yesterday.

She says how she forgot to text Anthony as the bus passed Alabang, that she couldn't concentrate on the movie because the cinema was jampacked, and that *The Kids Side* was playing the same song over and over.

"And this!"

Erika shows the envelope she got from Anthony.

"What's that?" asks Loris.

"Open it!" says Erika in reply.

Loris opens the envelope. She takes out the invitation

that is inside and reads it.

After reading the invitation, Loris looks at Erika and raises her eyebrows. Loris has this expression with her that says she's waiting for Erika to say something.

"Yeah! Anthony will be graduating from his master's studies next week, and we are invited."

"Wait! Come again. We?" Loris asks in disbelief.

"Yes, we! You and I! WE!" exclaims Erika.

"Are you out of your mind? Have you checked what day his graduation will be? It's Tuesday! How could we possibly attend? I have work. You have, too; even if you have a summer break in law school, that doesn't mean you have a break at work too." Loris says and glares at Erika.

"Of course, I checked! That's why I would use my vacation leave. I haven't used one since I started working at the company. It's about time for me to use it, don't you think?" Erika explains. She smiles and gives Loris a wink.

"You planned about this, don't you?" says Loris, grinning.

"Not really. How can I? I just got the invitation yesterday. What choice do I have?" replies Erika.

"Alright, I'll come with you. I will use one of my few but precious vacation leaves on that day. And it is only because you are my best friend. Of course, I want to meet Anthony again, too. I haven't seen him in ages!" agrees Loris.

Erika makes a sigh of relief.

"Thank you. I owe you one!" says Erika.

"It's nothing. You owe me nothing, Erika. I want to see you happy, and I mean it." Loris hugs her.

Erika smiles to her best friend, but there is a worried

expression on her face that makes Loris ask, “What is it?”

“I gave Anthony the poem I wrote.” Erika answers while in deep thought.

She wonders what Anthony’s reaction to the poem is. Erika wants to get her phone and call Anthony to ask him directly. But she controls herself. Erika knows that she can’t do it anyway.

“Really? The one you showed me before. What is the title again?” asks Loris.

“Yes. That one, ‘*Someone asked me*’. One of the few poems I have ever written,” replies Erika.

Erika smiles as she remembers the time she wrote that poem. It all started when an officemate, a guy, asked her if she had a boyfriend. Erika told her officemate ‘None’ but said that there is someone special to her. And Erika was thinking of Anthony at that time.

“Wait, one of the few poems? You mean you have more, but you didn’t show me,” says Loris.

She tries to look hurt but fails miserably.

“I wrote my second poem when I was in TLS, while I was reading some court reports. My other poems, I wrote them in between my second poem and now. I write poems when I am in the mood.” Erika defends herself.

“What was Anthony’s reaction? What did he say?” Loris asks. She really wants to know. She is curious!

“I don’t know,” says Erika and shrugs.

“Uhm, why you don’t know?” asks Loris.

“I gave it to Anthony before I went to the bus, and I did it on purpose because I am a coward! I don’t want to see his reaction,” explains Erika.

In the back of her mind, Erika wants to know Anthony's reaction. But she worries, too. Erika just can't say it out loud to Loris.

She prides herself on being very articulate. But right now, she can't articulate her worries and doubts to her best friend, even if she wants to.

"Have you heard from him?" Loris asks.

"No, not yet! That's why I need you to be with me at his graduation. I can't face him alone; not after I gave him the poem," answers Erika.

"Well, relax! I will accompany you to the graduation," says Loris. "And don't worry, as I recall, that poem of yours is OK and did not reveal anything at all. You didn't say that you were in love with him," says Loris.

She tries to make Erika feel better. Try is the word, but Loris thinks it didn't work.

Erika's face warms up a hundredfold as she hears her best friend mention being in love.

"Oooops! Don't try to deny it, Erika. It's all over your face. Just mentioning it makes you look like a full-ripe tomato!" Loris says.

Erika wants to deny it, but she just keeps her silence. She is not sure exactly what she's feeling. She misses Anthony and thinks of him all the time.

Is that love?

Erika has no idea at all.

Chapter 8

Six days later…

Erika checks her old personal email.

For the past few years, she hasn't received many important or personal emails. Most were about online marketing and commercial announcements.

All work-related emails are sent to her new email address, which was given to her when she started working at the company.

But meeting Anthony again awakens the feelings that she tried to hide, if not bury, for a long time.

She wants to go back to the old conversations that they had. To her shock and delight, there are two new messages from Anthony.

The first one has **Blooming** for a title, and the other one has **<no subject>** written on the subject area.

Erika stares at the screen for a second while deciding which of the two she will open and read first.

She then decides to open the one with the title.

Subject: Blooming

Dearest Erika,

I forgot to ask you if you are still using this email. I am taking my chances here and try to send this message anyway.

How are you? I really had a wonderful time with you last Saturday. Spending time with you is always a pleasure. As I have said, you are "blooming."

Is there someone special in your life now—someone reason enough to make you more and more beautiful? You sure have many admirers, and I am one of them.

By the way, I didn't know you wrote poems. I like the one you gave me. I put it into a frame and hung it on my bedroom wall.

See you next Tuesday!

Anthony

Erika read the email a couple of times. And every time, she's grinning from ear to ear.

It feels like college days.

Reading emails from Anthony brought back some memories.

Blooming and beautiful?

OMG!

Erika doesn't want to believe. Ever since, Erika has not been good at accepting compliments given to her.

Dearest?

When did he ever use that endearment for me before?

Never!

Why do you need to dissect everything that has been written and he had ever said to you?

Erika asked herself with a tone of reprimand. Erika wrote a simple and short reply to the email.

Subject: answer to your email

Anthony,

I opened my email after a long time of not doing so. That's why my reply is late. ☺ I seldom use it, but luckily today I did.

I'm glad to know that you like my first poem.

Yes, it's just my first try. I was inspired by your unfinished poem. See you on your graduation day!

Erika

Before sending her reply, Erika reads her message again, and then again, until she is convinced that it is OK. She didn't write anything about the "blooming" and "admirers" parts. She concentrated on her poem. When she is satisfied with what she has written, she hits send.

She then opens the other email. The email contains no written message, but there is an attachment to it. It is a word document with the filename: **The_song_of_my_heart.doc**.

Erika clicks and downloads the attached document.

The song of my heart

As the bird hums in the distance
And the stars shine above us
I can feel all my emotions
Swinging in just one direction

As I look at the perfect cone-shape
Of the town's majestic mountain
I can clearly picture you in my head
And how you make me dazzled

As the clouds touch and kiss
The beautiful mountain peak
I can't think of anything else
But this true love that I feel

As my stay nears the end
The moon above lights my way
I can clearly see the road I'll take
I hope it leads me to you one day

Erika can't believe what she is reading!

It was the one Anthony started writing when they were in Legazpi. She still has the piece of paper with the unfinished poem Anthony asked her to "keep safe."

Wow!

Just wow!

Erika is really in awe. She really thinks that Anthony is very creative, imaginative, and poetic.

He should be writing poems more often.

Erika then wonders who inspired Anthony to write this beautiful poem.

"*Who could possibly be his inspiration back then? He didn't tell me!*"

Well, they didn't have the same exact circle of friends in college.

I can't possibly know everyone, anyway, Erika thinks.

Erika was too timid to ask such a question before.

Should I ask him now?

Erika already sent a message to Anthony, so she doesn't want to send another one now.

Maybe I can ask him when we meet again.

After convincing herself, Erika opens her drawer and takes out the folder where she used to store important things. She opens it and takes a piece of paper. This is the second poem she wrote for Anthony.

She wanted to give this poem to Anthony along with the other she gave him, but she chickened out at the last minute and decided not to give it to him.

Now, she is contemplating including the second poem in Anthony's graduation gift.

She calls Loris.

This is to remind her best friend of Anthony's graduation on Tuesday. Erika already filed a two-day vacation leave at work, so she is ready. She finished most of her reports for the coming week. She only needs to do the last few on Monday and the rest when she comes back after her vacation leave.

It is almost eleven o'clock in the evening already, and she is still awake. She is supposed to be in bed by now, sleeping, and not thinking so much or stressing a lot. She should be making the most of the school vacation and recharging her energy.

But what can she do?

Her body is used to sleeping so late that it is still very much awake.

She decides to wrap the gift instead. It is a wristwatch. She chose the Voyage West Field Chronograph 43mm Stainless Steel Bracelet she saw at the mall the other day. She likes the silver metal color of the watch, which is why she chose it.

I hope Anthony will like it.

On Tuesday, Erika travels from Los Baños to Bucal via jeepney. Erika will meet her best friend at the corner of the street to Loris' subdivision. It is near the CU; that was why they both decided to just meet there and take the bus to Manila from that corner.

Loris is already waiting for Erika when she gets off the Jeep. They wait together for the bus.

It is Tuesday, so the traffic shall not be that bad. Erika prays that they will be able to make it to the graduation on time, as the bus takes time to arrive.

It is almost half past ten o'clock in the morning when

they finally sit on the bus. When Erika notices that the bus is going so slowly, she feels so nervous.

"Relax!" Loris says.

"How can I? We are going so slowly. The graduation is at two o'clock, and we are not even in Halang yet!" Erika replies in panic.

"OK. Will the bus go faster if you don't relax?" Loris asks Erika.

"And besides, the actual graduation is at three o'clock." Loris continues.

Well, Loris is right.

There will be a mass first at two o'clock, and then the graduation rite will follow. But still, she wants to be there earlier rather than later.

Is fate playing with me? Erika whispers.

At the rate at which the bus is moving, they will be in Manila later than they plan.

"It's unbelievable!" Erika exclaims.

"We are still in the Calamba area! We will not be able to reach graduation." Erika rants in frustration.

It is five minutes past twelve o'clock in the middle of the afternoon when their bus finally reaches the toll gate.

Erika can see from the bus front that the line going to Manila is unbelievably long. It adds to the frustration she's feeling right now.

Ding!

Erika hears her phone's message tone.

She knows, even before she looks at it, that the message is from Anthony.

And she is right!

Hey! Are you on the way! I am excited
to see you, and to graduate of course! ☺

"Was it from Anthony?" Loris asks her.

"Yes. What will I tell him?" Erika replies.

"Maybe you can just tell him that we are on our way; just a little bit of traffic at the moment," says Loris.

Erika types a message exactly as Loris suggested.

She omits to mention where they are. Anthony might be worried that they won't be able to make it.

It is half past one o'clock already, and the bus is still in the Susana Heights area in Sta. Rosa, Laguna.

Erika is now convinced that it is impossible for them to be at the graduation, which is set at two o'clock.

Yes, we're on our way! Just traffic!
See you in a bit. ☺

Erika crosses her fingers as she sends the message. She prays, too, that they will be able to make it to Anthony's graduation ceremony.

She is so anxious and nervous as she waits.

It is four o'clock in the afternoon when they reach the LRT Buendia station.

That says much about the traffic!

Ding!

It is a text message from Anthony. Erika opens her phone and reads the message.

> Where are you? Is everything OK?
> My graduation has just finished.

Anthony's graduation is an important milestone for him, and Erika knows it. He wanted her to be part of it but she didn't make it. It was not Erika's fault, but still, she couldn't calm herself. Erika is blaming herself for not being there for him.

> I'm sorry, we were caught in heavy
> traffic. We just reached LRT.

Not long after Erika sent her reply, another message from Anthony comes in.

> OK. Just come, and I'll wait for you.
> I'll be on the university signage with
> a big statue.☺

It is already five in the afternoon when they finally reach the university compound. Luckily, Loris knows the university well, so they are able to locate the place Anthony mentioned in his text easily.

They see Anthony right away. He is busy talking to someone on the phone. It gives Erika time to compose herself.

Anthony, Erika notices, is wearing a simple white long-sleeve polo, which he rolled up below his elbows. Anthony paired the polo with formal black pants and shoes that give him a very professional and composed look.

He has a very good posture—standing up so straight.

Even from a distance, he has this aura that exudes confidence, passion, and perseverance that Erika envies, too.

He is a personification of true grit!

Anthony turns and sees Erika and Loris as they approach him. He finishes his conversation with whoever is on the other line.

"You made it!" Anthony exclaims and smiles at them. But his gaze is more focused on Erika.

"Congratulations on your graduation, and sorry that we weren't able to see that," says Erika.

And for the first time, Erika initiates the hug. She hugs Anthony, and she feels wonderful doing so.

They hug for a couple of seconds until they hear Loris say, "Ehem! Ah guys, I am also here!" Loris teases them both and looks at them knowingly.

"Ooops, sorry! Hi, Loris. I'm glad you're able to come, too," says Anthony to Loris as he acknowledges her.

"Well, of course! I will not miss this moment." Loris waves her hands back and forth between Anthony and Erika.

Loris implies not the graduation but the reunion of the two, Erika and Anthony.

Erika blushes.

She is too embarrassed by what Loris is implying. Erika then gives Loris a warning stare. Loris ignores Erika; instead, Loris asks Anthony where his family are.

"My parents, together with my younger sister, are waiting for us in the restaurant. Juris and his family are there, too," replies Anthony.

He then continues, "I told them to go ahead because I will be waiting here for you two."

"You shouldn't have waited for us. You could have texted us where the restaurant is. We could have met you there instead." Erika says.

"It's no big deal, really. They have ordered for us. I hope it is OK for you both." Erika and Loris say OK almost in unison.

This makes the three of them laugh.

"Let's start moving then," says Anthony, and he takes Erika's hand and holds it.

Anthony starts walking in the direction of the university's multilevel car park, which is located near Lacson Avenue. Loris follows suit.

Chapter 9

"Mom, dad, remember Erika? She is my friend from Calamba University, and this is Loris, Erika's best friend." Anthony introduces them to his parents.

He then introduces them to his younger sister, Ana.

Erika and Loris say hello to them and shake their hands. Anthony's mom gives Erika a tight hug and smiles widely at her.

Anthony's looks are from his mom, and his posture is from his dad.

Erika thinks.

"I remember Erika! And how could I ever forget? Erika is the young, sweet, and smart lady, as you describe her, whom you keep on talking about the whole time you were at home," says Anthony's mom.

"Oh, my goodness, mom!" Anthony is surprised.

He is not expecting that from his mother.

He looks at Erika, and he sees that she is blushing. Anthony thinks Erika is prettier when blushing.

Juris laughs so hard from the other end of the table and says afterwards, "See, it is not just me! Tita also noticed."

"OK. I think that is enough. I don't know who's more embarrassed right now, Anthony or Erika. They are both red in their faces." It is Anthony's dad speaking.

His dad winks at Erika while patting his son's back.

"I am not blushing, dad!" Anthony says.

"Oh, you are, son. And it's OK," replies Anthony's dad.

Everyone on the table, including Erika and Loris, laughs with this banter between father and son.

They all sit and wait for their food.

Erika is seated beside Anthony. And on her left sits Loris.

"I'm sorry about that," whispers Anthony.

"About what?" Erika replies.

"About my mom and dad's teasing." Anthony says. He is embarrassed.

"Don't worry. It's OK." Erika is not going to admit that she was in fact a little embarrassed earlier when Anthony's mom mentioned him talking about her to his family.

At the same time, she feels a little bit thrilled.

Their food arrives.

Everyone starts eating, including Erika. She has no appetite for food, but she needs to eat. Sitting beside Anthony is making Erika nervous. She feels conscious, too, as his family looks at them so often.

Suddenly, a guitar is being played.

To everyone's surprise, a very popular singer and composer starts singing. She is also the one playing the guitar.

Erika listens as the singer sings the popular song "Pagdating ng panahon" (When the time comes). It is one of Erika's favorite songs. This song always touches Erika's heart whenever she hears it.

Erika feels every emotion the song wants to convey through the way the singer is singing it. It deepens its meaning.

Am I waiting for Anthony to notice me?

Am I waiting for him to love me?

If not now, maybe one day Anthony will come to his senses and love me the way I love him.

Erika finds herself asking, but only in her head. Erika sometimes wants to say yes to all the questions circling in her mind. But Erika knows that however much the sun rises and sets, they are just friends.

Only friends!

Will Anthony look and find me in his heart?

Erika wonders.

Erika's head is spinning right now. She's very much attuned to the song. She is basically dissecting it inside her head.

She wonders why every line of the song is like a prayer when she sings it.

Is she really hoping?

Am I being absurd by thinking all of these?

"What did you say?" Anthony asks Erika.

"Huh?" Erika feels confused at the question.

"I thought you were saying something," says Anthony.

Erika looks at Anthony and sees that he is staring at her, as if trying to find answers to some questions she has no idea about.

She shakes her head while smiling at him.

"I was just singing along, I think." Erika replies.

She's trying not to give Anthony any hint of what's going on in her mind. She just continues listening to the singer, and Anthony does the same.

Maybe it will happen, just not today.

Maybe one day.

Maybe.

Will it always be just a maybe between me and Anthony?

These thoughts linger in Erika's mind as the song reaches the end. Everyone claps their hands after the song, and the singer bows her head to the audience.

"I like that song," says Anthony, still clapping his hands and looking at the singer.

"I like it, too. She is brilliant with that song. She sang it well, too. It was so serene that I can feel it in my heart," answers Erika with much delight.

And it's true. Erika can feel every word.

"Were you two classmates in college?" Ana asks them.

This is after the applause subsides. Ana is sitting directly opposite Erika. Ana just looks at Erika without a trace of a smile at all.

"No, we were just schoolmates back then, and friends of course," answers Erika.

"Hey, Anthony, look! Finally, Iris is here!" says Ana to her brother.

She totally ignores Erika.

Ana stands up and greets the woman who just came in. They hug each other and kiss each other on the cheeks. Anthony stands up, too, and goes to the other side of the table to greet the woman.

Almost everyone on the table seems to know the woman, except Erika and Loris.

Anthony introduces Iris to Erika and Loris as a family friend who grew up also in Legazpi. Iris sits beside Anthony, while Juris moves to where Loris is sitting.

Feeling a little bit out of place suddenly, Erika excuses herself to go to the lady's room. And not long after, Loris comes and says, "It's getting hot in there!".

Loris winks at Erika.

"You seemed to be enjoying yourself very much. Tell me! What is the real score between you and Juris?" Erika asks Loris.

"He asked me out! Can you believe that?" Loris exclaims.

"I assumed, based on the excitement emanating from you, that you said yes," says Erika.

She smiles at Loris knowingly.

"Of course! Why would I not?" Loris replies, grinning.

"I didn't know you fancied Juris. You didn't say a thing about it before."

But before Loris can answer, Ana comes inside the lady's room. They both look at her and smile. Erika and Loris excuse themselves and goes out of the lady's room. They proceed to where they were seated before.

"Hey! There you are!"

Anthony smiles wide as he sees Erika approaches them again.

"I wonder where you have been," says Anthony.

"To the lady's room," answers Erika.

Juris calls Anthony and says something.

This gives Erika an opportunity to locate the gift she will give to Anthony in her bag. When she finds it, she happily looks up to Anthony.

"What?" Erika asks Anthony when she sees him staring at her.

"Nothing. I am glad that you celebrate this milestone with me." Anthony answers with a smile.

"Of course. That's what friends are for. Sharing successes, among others!" Erika answers.

"By the way, before I forget, here's my gift for you. Congratulations, again."

"You didn't have to give me a gift. Your presence is a gift for me already," replies Anthony.

"But I want to give it to you, so please do accept," says Erika while waiting for Anthony to accept the gift.

Anthony thanks her and accepts the gift.

"I think you two have no picture yet together. Would you mind if I take your picture before this evening ends?"

It is Loris talking to them.

"Sure. You can use my phone." Anthony replies.

Loris takes pictures of them using Anthony's phone. Loris takes another picture, but this time using Erika's digital camera. Erika has a digicam, which she got from her mother as birthday presents last year. She took it with her as she planned on taking pictures of Anthony's graduation. Since they were late, she forgot all about it until Loris mentioned it.

Everyone continues talking, laughing, and listening to the performer for the next 30 minutes. And when it is time for all of them to part ways, Anthony helps her to stand and holds her hand.

They are walking out of the restaurant still holding hands when Anthony says, "Juris could drive you and Loris home. They will be heading back to Laguna tonight anyway."

Erika timidly replies OK.

Everyone says their goodbyes to one another.

Anthony's mom hugs Erika and wishes her the best of luck in her law school. Erika says thank you, and she hugs Anthony's mother, too.

Before getting into the car, Anthony asks Erika to send a message when she gets home.

Erika nods.

They hug each other but they never say goodbye; instead, Anthony says, "Till next time, Erika. See you when I see you."

As Erika sits in the car, she sees Anthony walk towards Ana and Iris, who are waiting for him near the car Anthony used to get them to the restaurant earlier.

In the car, Erika is quiet.

Luckily, Loris and Juris are busy talking to each other. It gives Erika time to reflect and think over what happened to her day.

But not long after, Juris speaks louder than usual, as if he wants to engage Erika in the conversation.

"I thought it would be awkward when Iris came. In fact, I didn't expect she would be coming, really," says Juris.

He looks between Loris and Erika as he talks. Erika just listens. Knowing Juris, she knows there will be a follow-up to those statements.

"And why did you say that? Iris is a family friend. Wasn't that what Ana said?" Loris asks.

"Yes. She is. Ana and Iris are in fact the best of friends since they were in kindergarten. But..." Juris stops mid-sentence and looks at Erika.

Erika and Loris both wait for Juris to continue. Erika is not sure what she is expecting. She doesn't want to look so eager to hear what Juris is about to say. Erika has a hunch that it will not be good news for her. Erika gets nervous and starts freaking out.

When the silence becomes unbearable, it is Loris who asks Juris, "What? Will you please continue? What with the 'but'?"

Juris sighs.

Erika notices that Juris is struggling whether to say something or not. She actually feels pity for him, but at the same time, she is irritated at him for making her think of the worst and feel nervous.

Scratching his head, Juris says, "Well, I didn't know whether Anthony told you, Erika. And I shouldn't have started this."

"You are beginning to be annoying, Juris. Can you please stop this riddle and be straight to the point?" Loris tells Juris irritably.

"I'm trying!" Juris exclaims.

"Then try harder!" Loris says while she glares at Juris.

In Erika's peripheral vision, she can see Juris' parents looking at each other.

Are they wondering what is going on?

Juris seems annoyed at Loris, but more so at himself. He then says, "Iris is not just a family friend. She was in fact Anthony's ex-girlfriend. If I am not mistaken, they broke up six months ago."

This revelation stuns Erika.

She is not reacting at all. She is just waiting for Juris to retract what he had just said.

It can't possibly be true, can it?

Erika tries to remember if there was a time Anthony mentioned Iris to her.

Loris looks at Erika worriedly.

She then looks back at Juris and says, "You are joking, right?"

"I wish I was," replies Juris.

"Hey, are you OK?" Loris asks Erika.

"Yes. I am just wondering why Anthony didn't mention Iris before. But I guess it's none of my business anyway," says Erika.

She smiles at Loris and Juris, a smile that never reaches her eyes. She tries to be so loquacious as to hide what she truly feels at that moment.

But Erika fails on that task.

Maybe Anthony still has feelings for Iris; that is why he still invited her.

These thoughts are only in Erika's mind until Loris and Juris ask her in unison, "What did you say?"

"Huh?! I didn't say anything, did I?" Erika replies. Confused.

"You said something about Anthony and Iris," enlightens Loris.

OMG!

Did she say it out loud?

"Oh, don't mind me. I just remembered something, I guess." Erika says to them.

"And Juris, please don't tell Anthony that you told us about it. He will tell me, maybe, when he deems it necessary." Erika smiles at Juris.

Although deep inside, she's hurting.

She doesn't have the right, and Anthony doesn't have to tell her if he doesn't want to.

We are just friends and nothing more.

So why am I hurting?

Erika doesn't know why she's feeling like this.

Juris nods.

Loris and Juris stay quiet for a while. They let Erika process everything in silence.

Erika looks outside the window and prays that they will be able to get home soon.

Very soon!

She wants to be alone.

Chapter 10

"Why do you look so sad? You should be enjoying." Anthony hears her sister, Ana.

Anthony is in Intramuros, Manila, with his sister Ana and Iris. They are inside a bar with a very nice deck that can see the sky and the city skyline.

They went there right after his graduation dinner.

It has been two hours since they came to the bar. And now Anthony is eager to get back to his apartment.

He doesn't really want to go out tonight, not without Erika anyway. But he can't ask Erika to stay. It will be late for her to travel back to Laguna. Anthony was grateful when his cousin Juris volunteered to drive Erika and Loris home.

He just borrowed her sister's car. Anthony's own car is in Legazpi. He doesn't like driving in Manila. He's used to commute.

"I'm tired. It has been a long day," replies Anthony.

Her sister raises her eyebrows.

Anthony ignores it.

Iris is out talking to someone on the phone. This gives Anthony and her sister a little time to talk.

"I didn't know you'd invite Iris. You didn't tell me." Anthony continues.

"Why? Is there a problem?" Ana asks.

"Yes. It caught me by surprise, to say the least." It was unexpected, and he didn't like it, not at all.

“I thought it would be better for you and Iris to talk. Iris seemed sad after you two broke up,” says Ana.

She seems proud of herself for doing something for her brother and Iris.

“You don’t have to mediate between us. We are OK. I know what you’re doing. You are forcing us to be together again.” Anthony tells his sister.

He can’t control his irritation towards his sister.

For the last couple of months, her sister has been nagging him to call Iris.

Anthony had already told his sister on a few occasions to stay away from his personal affairs, especially his relationship with Iris.

But it seems that she is not getting the memo.

His sister and Iris have been best friends since they were in grade school. Anthony understands that her sister wants Iris for him.

But it is not as simple as that.

“Iris is going back to Legazpi, maybe for good. And you are coming back too. So, what’s the problem? Isn’t it better if you and her can patch things up?” Ana tells him.

Anthony knows all about it, of course.

During his relationship with Iris, she’s been talking about moving back to her hometown for good. When they parted ways, Anthony wished Iris the best of luck.

Anthony, on the other hand, has an ongoing discussion with his family about him coming back to Legazpi. Anthony wants to pursue law, and his dad supports this.

Since he became friends with Erika, the direction Anthony wanted to go has changed. His family is very supportive of all his plans. His dad told him to study law after he finishes his master's degree. Anthony can study law and become a lawyer.

The only problem now, and this is what makes Anthony's mind restless, is that his dad asked him if he could take it in UL instead of in Manila.

This means he will be far away from Erika again.

They just recently reconnect with each other after many years of not seeing one another, and now Anthony might be leaving Erika again.

"Hello! Penny for your thoughts!" Anthony hears her sister. She is also snapping her fingers in front of him.

Anthony didn't know how long he had been drifting from their conversation, and he doesn't care at all. He is busy thinking about the way he will talk to Erika.

"Can you stay away from my personal affair, will you? Please?" Anthony asks his meddling sister.

"My personal life is complicated already. I don't want your meddling to make it more complicated. You have no idea what's really going on between me and Iris. So please, leave my personal life alone." Anthony continues.

Ana is on the verge of saying something but stops as she sees Iris on her way back to their table.

"Sorry about that. It was work." Iris explains.

"I think I have to call it a night. They need some reports for tomorrow, and I have to prepare for it," continues Iris.

"It's OK. We'll drive you home, Iris." Ana volunteers.

Ana looks at Anthony with an expression that tells him that their conversation is not over yet.

Anthony can't thank enough the heavens, or perhaps

the one who called Iris earlier for this sudden halt on their night out.

He doesn't need to stay longer at the bar. He can finally go back to his apartment and dwell on the things that really matter to him right at that moment.

They get out of the bar.

Anthony drives both her sister and Iris to their separate homes. He then commutes back to his apartment by taking an Uber. Ana needs her car tomorrow, so he can't borrow it again.

Back at his apartment, Anthony takes a shower and then gets ready to bed.

He didn't lie to his sister when he said he was tired. But sitting at the bar, talking to her sister and Iris while his mind was so far away, literally drained him.

But even if he is tired, he can't seem to sleep. His mind keeps traveling back to Erika.

Anthony gets off the bed and walks toward his study table, where he put all the gifts he had received today. He picks up the gift he got from Erika. Anthony then returns to his bed, sits there, and looks at the gift contemplatively.

I will open the gift before I sleep.

All the other gifts he received from his family, friends, and relatives can wait until tomorrow morning.

Anthony's tiredness is instantly gone.

He is now excited to know what can possibly be inside the box. Though Anthony finds it strange that the gift has no card attached to it.

He looks at the box from different angles. He is trying to see if there's any handwritten message, or something like '*To Anthony, From Erika'*, but finds nothing at all.

Now, curiosity is beginning to creep in.

He opens the box and finds two things inside.

The first one is another box, with silver text embossed on top. He opened the box and was surprised to see a stylish, silver metal-colored wristwatch.

Anthony has an instant like on the watch.

He takes the watch out of the box and tries it.

It is a perfect fit.

I need to call Erika.

Anthony reaches for his phone, but before he dials Erika's number, he looks at his new wristwatch and sees that it is very late in the evening.

Anthony knows that Erika is home already. She got home safely. Juris sent him a message earlier to tell him about it.

Erika promised me she will send a message when she gets home. Did she forget?

Maybe she is tired and sleeping already.

Anthony says to himself.

I will text and see if she will reply.

Hey. Are you still awake? Can I
call you? ☺

He waits for Erika's reply.

But after 10 minutes without receiving anything, he decides to call in the morning instead.

The second item in the gift box is a roll of papers with a ribbon.

It looks like a diploma.

Anthony takes it out of the box and opens it.

The first roll of paper has a poem written on it. The other one is a letter. Both are handwritten on a very elegant type of paper. Anthony is so impressed, to say the least.

Anthony himself is so lazy to write by hand in most circumstances, and knowing Erika made a tremendous effort for his graduation gift makes him more impressed and surprised at the same time.

They are beautifully and carefully handwritten.

He reads the poem first and smiles. He will frame the poem and hang it on the wall.

Maybe I will start collecting Erika's poem on this wall.

Anthony smiles on that thought. As he reads the poem, a thought comes into his mind.

Shouldn't I be the one giving this poem to Erika? This poem captured what I have been feeling ever since Erika and I became friends.

Love and Reason

How beautiful it is to love someone
Without thinking of anything in return
Let the feelings and emotions flow
Thoughts and logic will soon follow

Even if some moments are not enough
There's something to be thankful and glad
The way love is being written and given
It is ok and maybe label doesn't matter

Sometimes all it needs is a sweet smile
For emotions to grow a thousand miles
This is the power of a flexible heart
It makes someone be gentle and kind

Happiness in love is not guaranteed
And love can make the heart bleeds
For love is so complex and defies logic
The heart has its reasons usually unique

Can the heart and mind work together?
Is blending feelings and thoughts clever?
Maybe it can make someone stronger
Or perhaps can lead to a total disaster

Erika is always full of surprises, and I am in full admiration every time.

He reads the poem over and over, as if trying to memorize every word.

Anthony can picture Erika saying all those words to him, trying her best to make him understand the importance of balancing the mind and the heart.

Can Erika possibly know about my dilemma?

After Anthony finishes reading the poem for the nth time, he then reads the letter that accompanies the poem next.

Anthony,

Congratulations!

It was a surprise to me when you told me you were graduating from your master's degree. We didn't communicate much for years, and I didn't know you went back to the university. Anyway, I am proud of you and thankful that you made me part of this milestone.

I noticed that you are still wearing the same wristwatch you had since college. I don't know the story behind the watch. But after I saw the wristwatch, I thought of you. I think it suits you well.

I know you like to write poems. But this time, I want to give you my poem, "Love and Reason." This was just my second poem.

So, maybe you are wondering why **Love and Reason***?*

Well, I was reading the SCRA when I stumbled upon a controversial case in which the Supreme Court cited the quote of Blaise Pascal about heart and reason upon ruling. I thought it would be great for me to write a poem about logic and emotion.

And here it is 'Love and Reason'.

I am giving it to you as a gift with the hope that you will like it as much as I do.

Now it's not mine anymore, but rather yours.

N.B.
Please be gentle with your criticism of that poem because my brain could only take a little of it, and my heart could break into pieces!

Erika

He can't imagine the time and effort Erika used to write this letter by hand. It seems written very carefully and intricately.

"I find it very sexy," whispers Anthony.

Anthony can't help but admire Erika more.

She's truly amazing!

Anthony smiles.

He wishes to talk to Erika, or better hugs her right now.

Criticism?

There's nothing to criticize about.

This is what lingers in Anthony's head. He really likes the poem.

Anthony sighs.

He really needs to find the balance between logic and emotion, or, as Erika puts it, "Love and Reason."

He takes off the wristwatch and places it back in its box. He rolls the poem and the letter again, but he fails tremendously with the ribbon, so he just gives up.

He will put the poem into the frame tomorrow, anyway. This is what's going on in Anthony's mind as he places the gift box on the table beside the bed.

Chapter 11

Erika wakes up at around one o'clock in the afternoon the following day. She is feeling so drained and tired.

She doesn't know what time she fell asleep the night before.

Thank God I applied for two days off.

When she applied for a vacation leave, she filed for two days because she doesn't know what time she will be home.

It was a smart decision on her part because, in her condition and state of mind, she's not fit to work today.

She remembers that Anthony sent her a message asking her if she was still awake last night.

She was!

She was crying, and she didn't want him to know. So, she just ignored it and pretended that she was already sleeping.

It was already twilight, as Erika remembers, and her tears were still pouring from her eyes. Sleep was nowhere in sight for her. She was assessing her feelings the whole night.

Erika has kept telling herself that she has no right to feel hurt or to feel whatever she's feeling.

Erika and Anthony are friends, nothing more and nothing less.

Erika can't expect Anthony to tell her everything about his life.

She wonders how long Anthony and Iris were together

before they called it quit. Anthony and Iris recently broke up, or at least six months ago; this was according to Juris.

Erika had no idea what's going on in his personal and professional life until they met a week ago.

Was it Iris the reason why Anthony seldom sent me a message for these past years?

Erika tries to remember how they started communicating again.

She received a call from Anthony one day in April of this year, and this shocked her to say the least. She didn't expect it at all.

Later, that same day, she got a message from Loris to tell Erika that Juris was asking for Erika's new number. Juris explained to Loris that it was Anthony who wanted it.

Erika lost her phone last year, so Erika had to change her number. So, if Anthony was sending Erika a text or was trying to call her at that period, then Erika was definitely not getting them.

At the same time, Erika seldom opens her personal emails. She's been busy with work.

Erika gets off of the bed and walks straight to the mirror to see how she looks before going out of her room. Her eyes are very swollen.

This is why she seldom cries, or at least tried to not cry. Her eyes swell so easily.

Erika sighs.

How can I go out of my room looking like this?

Mom would notice my swollen eyes.

But before she can go out of her room, her phone rings. A song started playing. She can hear her favorite foreign band singing. It only means that it's Anthony.

But where did I put my phone?

Erika is trying to squeeze her brain out. Her phone is nowhere in sight.

Before the song reaches the chorus, Erika finds her phone in her bag.

Erika inhales and exhales two times before she answers the call.

"Hello," says Erika timidly.

"Hello, Erika! Am I disturbing you?" Anthony asks.

"Not really. I just woke up," replies Erika.

How are you?

Did you go out last night after dinner?

I heard you just broke up with Iris. How come you didn't tell me?

These are what Erika really wants to ask Anthony. She will sound like a jealous girlfriend if she asks, so she just shuts up.

"You mean you didn't go to work today? That's good. How was your trip back home last night? Was it traffic again?"

Anthony is firing her too many questions, and Erika rolls her eyes. She is really trying not to talk much, but Anthony is making it difficult for her to keep quiet.

"Nope. I took two days off. Our trip last night was smooth. No traffic whatsoever." Erika replies.

"Anyway, is that why you call? To ask me about the traffic last night?" Erika is trying to make a light conversation by teasing Anthony.

Love and reason, Erika–remember love and reason.

Erika convinces herself, or is trying to convince herself,

that she can control her emotions by concentrating on the facts at hand.

Isn't she learning that the weight of reasons and emotions is just the same?

She must learn to balance the two so as not to outweigh one and the other.

If I want to be a lawyer, I shouldn't be too emotional. I must always stay with the facts.

Erika reminds herself.

Anthony laughs.

At least I can make you laugh.

"OK, seriously, what made you call me today? Did I forget something?" She asks.

"Nope. I would just like to thank you for your gifts."

"You are very much welcome."

Was Iris your inspiration when you wrote the poem in Legazpi, way back in college? The one that made you dazzled. And who was that 'true love' you have found?

These are the questions that Erika wants to ask, but as usual, she doesn't have the courage to do so.

But again, Anthony might think that Erika is fishing for information if she asks all those questions.

So, No!

She won't ask.

"I really like the watch. It fits perfectly on me." Anthony says.

He then continues, "And the poem is now hanging on my wall. I think I will start collecting your poems."

"Well, it will be a very few collections, then."

Erika smirks even if Anthony can't see her.

"Seriously, you have made me contemplate. I really liked it. And not only that, but you also inspired me to write more poems."

Erika has the luxury of blushing after hearing Anthony admit that she inspired him. He can't see her anyway.

Erika tries to change the topic.

She doesn't want them to focus much on the "inspiration thing" Anthony was talking about.

She is not comfortable talking about it.

"Thank you. But how come you call me in the middle of the day? Don't you have work?" Erika asks.

"I actually took one week of my vacation leave. I have tons of things to do. I won't be able to concentrate at work anyway until I finish all things not related to work," explains Anthony.

"Oh, I see. Good for you. You deserve it after all the hard work you put into your studies. What is your plan anyway?"

Erika feels the serene emotion suddenly enveloping her as she continues talking with Anthony.

"I haven't decided yet, or at least it is not yet final. For now, all I can say is that I am in the middle of the crossroads."

Erika hears Anthony sigh.

This only means that something is bothering him.

Erika hears Anthony continues on the other line, "I emailed a poem to you last night. I can't sleep after I read your letter and poem. As I have said, your poem and letter made me reflect and contemplate. At the same time, you are inspiring me."

What can I say?

You inspired me too!

That's what Erika wants to say, but instead she says, "Thank you. I am humbled."

I am humbled.

What kind of reply was that?

Erika wants to kick herself.

Here she goes again!

She feels like a weirdo when she is talking with Anthony.

Where is the loquacious Erika?

Erika is calm earlier, but she realizes now that her calm is in a temporary hibernation.

"Maybe we can go out again. I will be in Laguna this weekend. I will be staying at Juris. I will send you a message before then. My dad is calling, so I have to end the call. See you when I see you, Erika." Anthony tells her.

Anthony seems in a hurry, so Erika just says OK.

Instead of going out of the room, Erika goes back to bed with her phone in her hand. She closes her eyes and thinks of what happened right there and then.

I inspired him!

Me?

Erika has difficulty believing it.

Why can't I just accept the compliment?

Her head is spinning thinking so much about it. Erika didn't write in her letter that she was thinking of Anthony when she wrote the poem.

Yes.

Erika was fascinated by the court ruling; that was why she was able to write that poem.

But if Erika is being honest with herself, she knows that it was just half the truth. Her inspiration in writing that poem was, in fact, Anthony.

Because during the time when Erika was in a rush to finish the reading assignment and report, her mind was occupied by the thought of Anthony.

And Anthony alone!

And I will not admit that to him!

Erika is still clutching the phone when she hears the message alert sound.

She looks at it and sees that the message is from Anthony.

As I threaded the path of life,
A realization dawns on me.
Balancing the mind and heart,
Is the hardest part of the journey!
-Anthony-

Exactly!

This is exactly what I had in mind when I wrote the poem, Love and Reason.

Erika types a reply.

Hey. You have captured the essence
of my poem in a quatrain. I am so
impressed! ☺

She reads the message twice before sending.

And not long after she sends the message, her phone

'dings' again. It is a reply from Anthony.

"Huh, that is super quick," says Erika to herself.

Hey. I told you; I was inspired! ☺

Erika smiles.

She feels lighter now than last night.

She is thankful that Anthony called her. It helped her a lot in dealing with her emotions. His voice was like a cure to her broken heart.

Yes, she felt heartbroken last night for whatever reason she still can't figure out.

Erika stands up, combs her hair, and changes her clothes. She puts her phone in her bag before she goes out of her room. Erika walks straight to the kitchen, as she is so hungry.

Scratch that!

I.am.starving!

Erika needs food in her stomach to regain the energy she lost from crying and the heavy drama she put herself through last night.

Admittedly, it was her own doing. And Erika has only herself to blame!

I can't blame Anthony for it.

Luckily, her mother is out talking to their neighbor. This gives Erika the time to eat her "brunch" without having to explain to her mother why her eyes are swollen.

After eating, she washes her dishes and goes to the bathroom to shower.

Back to her room, Erika checks if there is a message.

None.

She opens her laptop and checks her emails.

Erika checks first her work email. Even if she is on leave, she needs to check if there's an important message she has to attend to.

Thank God there's no email!

Her sighs of relief are very evident.

She then opens her personal email.

Erika can see that she received an email from Anthony. She already forgot about it, but Anthony mentioned the poem he emailed to her when they were talking earlier.

She was so busy feeling all the emotions that bombarded her, and she was trying to come to terms with the compliments Anthony gave her that Erika forgot about the email.

The subject of the email message is **Poem.**

This doesn't give Erika any idea of what the poem is all about.

She excitedly opens the email.

There is a short message to it and an attached document. The attached file, like the other one before, is a Word document file.

The name of the file is:

The_path_I_always_dreamed_of.doc

Subject: Poem

Dear Erika,

You inspired me to write this one.

I don't have that sexy and elegant handwriting like yours, so I have to type it instead. ☺

It will be a shame if you can't read the poem just because of my terrible penmanship. ☺

See you when I see you. ☺

Anthony

Sexy?

My handwriting is not sexy!

Erika is screaming inside her head after reading the sexy word.

OK, I have a fine penmanship, but not sexy!

She has a lot of compliments about her handwriting before. No one, but no one used the term sexy to describe her handwriting.

Erika laughs and blushes at the same time, as a thought creeps into her mind.

Why can't Anthony just write that I have good penmanship and that I am sexy?

Her eyes tear up from laughing hard at her own joke.

You?

Sexy?

Keep on dreaming, Erika!

Keep on dreaming!

When her laughter subsides and she gets back her composure, she opens the attached file. It takes a while before the attached file downloads and opens.

While waiting, Erika contemplates.

Hmmm?

The path I always dreamed of.

What can it possibly be?

Erika is dying to know what the path is.

So, Anthony has been dreaming of this, whatever it is, all this time.

She wonders what it is.

The path I always dreamed of

As I walk down the silent street
The time when day and evening kiss
A thought creeped into my mind
I can't wait long for another twilight

You have shown me the way
To the path where I should go
And it leads me down the road
I dreamed a long time ago

I saw that dream in a reflection
Or was it just a fragment of imagination?
The image seems more of a gray
Than a clear black and white on a day

Should I dare continue walking alone
And follow the path where I belong
This very thought gives me a fright
Hitting directly my fragile heart!

Indecision is driving me to the brink
A world no one knows but me, I think
I should hit the ground running soon
Before the sun is gone replace by the moon

Erika stares at the screen in front of her.

Just stares.

She is trying to figure out what the poem is telling her. Since she knows Anthony very well, it is an expression of what he feels and thinks.

What was the path he was talking about?

And who showed him the way?

Erika wonders.

Erika just can't possibly assume that it is her the poem refers to, even if Anthony wrote in the message that she inspired him to write the poem.

How can I?

Erika doesn't have any idea what path Anthony is talking about in the poem.

Erika's head begins to spin.

She tries to squeeze her brain for an answer.

The logical part of Erika's brain is telling her that '*inspiring*' Anthony to write the poem doesn't necessarily mean that the poem is about *her*.

It is possible that Anthony meant *her writings*.

And the emotions, as well as Anthony's dreams, which he had been keeping to himself for a long time, were triggered by what Erika wrote in her letter and maybe in her poem 'Love and Reason', too.

Dare walking alone?

Why?

What does it mean?

These are some of the questions Erika is pondering in her head.

Where he belongs?

What?

Erika doesn't understand.

Is he saying goodbye now?

Sometimes, being too logical is a curse for her.

Why can't she just simply enjoy the poem?

She doesn't need to dissect and interpret every single word written in the poem.

But there's a message in the poem, and Erika needs to figure it out!

And deep inside, she wants the poem to be about her.

Yes!

She can't deny it any longer.

She wants Anthony to notice her. Not just as his friend, but more than that.

Erika has no experience in the love department. She's single forever.

Erika smiles when she remembers the common joke she and her classmates have in law school about them being single.

Most women in their class are single and have never

been in a relationship.

That is why they started this group, which they called *'Soltera ab initio'*.

Soltera is a Latin word that means single, and *ab initio* means from the beginning.

So, it is not surprising that Erika is not used to this kind of emotion she's feeling lately; she is after all *soltera ab initio*.

Chapter 12

Afraid to say what we feel
The summer wind sends a chill
Not ready to go the distance
And ruin what we have now

The rest of the week goes by smoothly and uneventfully for Erika. She is at work from eight in the morning until around five o'clock in the afternoon.

She doesn't go out with friends or whatsoever every after working hours.

Erika sends a text message to Loris and asks her if Loris wants to eat out, but unfortunately, she rains checked. Loris says she has to work overtime.

Not even on a freaking Friday night!

Erika rolls her eyes.

Anthony hasn't texted her either, so she doesn't know if he will be coming or not.

She patiently waits for his message. Erika has no idea when Anthony will be coming.

Can it be today?

Or maybe tomorrow?

Sunday perhaps?

Or maybe not at all.

Erika sighs.

She can't do anything but wait.

Erika can feel that her patience is getting the better of her. She doesn't bargain for this waiting game.

This is definitely not sitting well with her.

As boredom starts to creep in, Erika plays with her phone. She scrolls it up and down a couple of times. She looks at all her contacts on the phone.

When she sees Anthony's name, she decides to change the saved name.

Erika smiles and feels satisfied after doing so.

"Erika, dinner is ready!" Erika hears her mother call her.

She goes out of her bedroom. She doesn't really have the appetite for food, but her mother prepares dinner for the two of them. Erika doesn't want to disappoint her mother.

It isn't often that she eats dinner at home with her mother. Erika has to work overtime on weekdays and usually eats in the company canteen.

During weekends, Erika ordinarily comes home late from Manila and has already eaten.

So this is actually a rare occasion for the two of them to eat together.

"I prepared your favorite, pork kaldereta," says her mother as Erika sits beside her.

"Thanks mom," says Erika and smiles.

Erika is forever thankful for having a mother like her.

They eat while they talk about the coming school year. Erika will be in her second year of law school. She will be busy again.

Her mother doesn't complain about it, though.

She knows how important it is for Erika to pursue her dream. It doesn't mean that her mother is not worried about Erika.

Her mother used to tell Erika that she is so focused on her career and pursuing her dream that she has no social life anymore.

"Is that the sound of our doorbell or the sound of your phone?" Her mother asks Erika suddenly.

The sound is so low that Erika has difficulty hearing it. They keep silent and try to listen attentively.

"Breathless!" Erika exclaims.

"What breathless?" Her mother asks. Confused.

"It's my phone ringing, mom." She answers her mother.

Based on her mother's expression, she still doesn't understand what Erika meant by breathless.

Erika runs to her room to answer the call.

"Hello!" says Erika, a little breathy from the adrenaline.

"Hi, Erika," replies Anthony.

Erika didn't say anything. She stays quiet and waits for Anthony to say more.

"Am I bothering you? Are you busy?" Anthony asks.

"Nope. Not at all. I just finished dinner with my mom." She answers.

"Actually, we are outside of your house," says Anthony.

"We? Outside of our house? You mean outside, as in outside of our house. Here in Los Baños?" Erika knows she is babbling, and her confidence is hiding.

She hears Anthony laugh.

Yeah right!

Keep on babbling, Erika!

She wants to kick herself for losing her calm and control again.

Why is it that when I am talking with Anthony, I feel

like I am different?

She hears Anthony say, "Yes. We are outside. Loris, Juris, and yours truly! We are picking you up."

Erika goes out of her room.

She tells her mother that her friends are outside. Erika is still holding her phone when she goes out of their house to open the gate.

"What's with the surprise?" Erika asks.

She looks back and forth between the three of them. She then continues, "Loris, you said you have overtime; that's why we can't go out for dinner."

Erika looks questioningly at her best friend.

"My boss decided that it could wait until Monday. I should have called you. But before I was able to, Juris called me and told me that we would all go out together," explains Loris.

"Erika! Who are you talking to?" Erika's mother calls her.

Ooops. She forgot her manners!

"Oh, I'm sorry. Please come in." Erika says.

When they are all seated on the sofa, Erika excuses herself to tell her mother why her friends pay them a visit.

She then goes to her room to change her clothes and get her handbag.

"Maybe you can overnight at my apartment." Loris says to Erika.

"Why?" Erika asks Loris.

"It would be fun. We have all the time tonight to talk. I miss our talks." Loris replies.

Erika's mother agrees to what Loris had just said.

"That's a wonderful idea! You should do that, Erika."

Erika looks at Anthony and Juris.

They were both just listening to their conversation. She excuses herself again to get more things.

She is a little stressed.

Erika is very organized and always wants to be in control. So, this sudden plan is getting on Erika's nerve.

A little heads up could have been great.

Erika thinks that it's good that she never tells her mother about her feelings for Anthony. She doesn't want to give her mother false hope.

Erika might love Anthony, but that doesn't mean that Anthony loves her the way she loves him. It will be more difficult to explain to her mom if she knows Erika's feelings for him.

They drove all the way to Nasugbu Highway in Tagaytay. Juris wants a beer and pizza, and he says he knows a place. It is a long drive, but luckily and surprisingly, the traffic isn't that heavy.

It is half past nine in the evening when they reach their destination, Your Best Pizza Bar. It was Erika's first time to be in this pizza bar. The place is good and clean.

The place is already full of customers when they come. Most of them seem to come directly from work, and they are now taking the Friday night out.

Juris gets them a nice table, located beside the window. Juris knows the owner and had called him before hand to make sure they have a good place when they come.

The view is absolutely fantastic.

It is worth the long drive.

Erika looks outside, and she feels so amazed, because from where she is seated, Erika can see the Taal volcano, the smallest active volcano in the world.

Anthony asks Erika what she likes to eat. Since she just had dinner when they picked her up, she's not that hungry. She just told Anthony that she will only have a Caesar salad and a glass of mango juice.

The other three order pizza, mango-shrimp salad, crispy fried chicken, and pesto pasta. Only Juris and Loris order a glass of beer each. Anthony orders just a sparkling water for a drink since he will be the one driving back to Laguna.

While they are eating, they talk about different things. Juris keeps his promise of not mentioning to Anthony that Erika knew about him and Iris.

It is ten o'clock in the evening when they finally get out of the pizza bar. But instead of going to the car, Loris suggests that they go down to what seems like a "view deck" of sorts.

Loris and Juris go straight to the left corner to see the Taal volcano. While Erika and Anthony just sit in one of the benches. This gives the two of them time to talk.

"I never thought I would be in Tagaytay this evening," says Erika.

"Me, too, in fact." Anthony says.

He then tells Erika that when he came to Laguna, Juris had another plan. Anthony and Juris picked Loris up from her work, and then they drove to Erika's house to pick her up, too.

"Why did you come to Laguna, anyway?"

"I want to visit you. I thought we can spend some time

together since we didn't have much time lately. I want to catch up with the lost time." Anthony replies.

He is looking at Erika as he speaks.

"Wow! Really?" Erika asks in disbelief.

Anthony stares at her and then smiles. He then asks, "Don't you believe me?"

Erika didn't answer. She just stares back at Anthony.

"Have you read the poem I emailed you?" Anthony remembers to ask Erika.

He then continues, "You didn't reply to my email, so I don't know whether you have read it, or worse, you haven't received it."

Erika is torn between asking all the questions she has after reading the poem two days ago or just playing it safe.

"Yes," she answers.

Erika doesn't elaborate her answer. She buys her time to come up with a question.

"And?" Anthony waits for her to say more.

"What was the path you were talking about?" Finally, Erika had the courage to ask Anthony.

Erika tries so hard to decode the message Anthony wants to convey to her through his poem for the past two days. She has been restless, and yet she is still unsure of what Anthony is trying to tell her.

So, she decides to stop squeezing her brain out and just ask Anthony.

He wanted to tell me something, wasn't he?

Why would he send me the poem if that was not his intention?

This is what's going through Erika's mind as she waits

for Anthony's reply.

"I am thinking about studying law. Just like you." Anthony replies.

Erika notices that even if Anthony smiles as he says that, there is a hint of sadness in his eyes.

Is it just my imagination?

"Wow! That's great!" Erika means it.

She always believes that Anthony can strive for everything he wants.

I always believe that Anthony is a man of grit!

Erika has no doubt about it.

"I haven't fully decided yet. The poem and the letter you gave me on my graduation awakened that dream I had for a long time."

As Anthony speaks, he is looking directly into Erika's eyes, as if he is trying to know what's on her mind.

"It was not my intention to put you on the brink, as it says on the last stanza," says Erika.

From the outside, she looks calm and composed, but deep within her, there's this turmoil and nagging feelings she can't get out of her system.

"Hey, don't beat yourself up. It wasn't you that put me on the brink. It was my indecisiveness. You inspire me, Erika. And I want you to remember that."

Anthony smiles without a hint of sadness this time.

"Why the indecision, then? You said it yourself. It has always been your dream."

Anthony doesn't reply.

He just stares at Erika. He is trying to find the answer to that question through her.

"By the way, what's my name on your phone? I keep wondering about that for a long time now," says Anthony, changing the subject.

"Isn't it your name, Anthony?" Erika teases.

Anthony laughs at that. He doesn't press her.

"Hey loved birds. Aren't you two going to enjoy the view? Are you both going to just sit there?" Anthony and Erika both turn their heads towards the voice.

It is Juris who says that.

He is grinning from ear to ear, while Loris is laughing beside him.

"You mind your own business! They don't need the view. They are busy. Let them be!" Loris to Juris.

Although Erika and Anthony can hear Loris from a distance.

"Don't mind him. He's just being annoying as usual." Loris shouts to Anthony and Erika.

And they all laugh.

Erika and Anthony look at each other.

Without saying a word, they both stand up and walk with their hands locked in each other towards the direction where Juris and Loris are standing.

Anthony holding Erika's hand is becoming natural for them. She is becoming accustomed to it.

Juris and Loris look at each other as Anthony and Erika approach them. They try to ignore the fact that Anthony and Erika are holding hands while walking.

Yes, they can try ignoring us, but they are failing miserably.

She grins, and she too tries to ignore Juris and Loris!

They all have fun reminiscing about the past, especially their college years, while they are looking at the view from a distance.

It is near midnight when they decide to leave the place.

As they go towards the parking area, Anthony borrows Erika's phone. She gives it to him, though she wonders what he will do about it.

Erika sees that Anthony also takes out his phone, and then he dials a number.

The song "Breathless" fills the air.

OMG!

Erika totally forgets that Anthony can check his number by dialing hers.

His name will be flashing on her phone's screen. She just recently changed Anthony's name, and now she regrets doing so.

Can the earth just open and swallow me, please?

Erika prays.

But why is she feeling weird right now?

Shy but thrilled!

Chapter 13

"Spill the beans!" Loris says.

Erika and Loris are getting ready to go to bed. It was a tiring day, and yet they had a fun evening with Juris and Anthony to end it.

The guys drove Erika and Loris to Loris' subdivision, where Loris is renting an apartment.

As "planned," Erika will sleep over there.

And Loris, being Loris, wants to know about what's going on between Erika and Anthony.

It will be a long night.

And sleep might be far from the agenda tonight.

"What are you talking about?"

Erika feigns innocence.

"Oh, come on! Don't try feigning innocence on me. It won't work, Erika. I know you better than you know yourself sometimes," says Loris with raised eyebrows.

The look Loris is giving Erika at that moment is telling her that Erika can try to contradict her, but it won't change a thing.

Erika sighs.

She knows Loris is right.

Lately, she doesn't really know herself, most especially when it comes to Anthony.

"OK. What do you want to know?" Erika asks.

"Why don't you start with what happened to you last

Tuesday? When Juris told us about Iris and Anthony, you looked like your puppy was being hit by a car! I was so worried!" Loris replies.

"Really?" Erika asks in disbelief.

She can't imagine what she looked like last Tuesday.

"Yes. You were as white as a ghost. And there was a moment when I thought that you weren't breathing. I called Juris the day after to scold him!" Loris says.

She looks at Erika with concern in her eyes.

"I was just temporarily shocked. That's all." Erika explains.

"I got that vibe. That was why I elbowed Juris so he wouldn't say more that could upset you." Loris looks at Erika with much understanding this time.

Erika smiles and says, "Thank you, Loris. You've been such a true friend to me since day one."

And Erika means it.

Loris always got her back. As in always!

"Have you asked Anthony about it? Did you confront him?" Loris asks.

Erika is horrified by what Loris asked her.

Confront Anthony?

Hell, NO!

The thought of confronting Anthony is beyond imaginable.

She says to Loris, "NO! Why would I do that? Anthony doesn't owe me anything. He doesn't need to tell me about his relationship with Iris or with any other woman! I am not his girlfriend, Loris. Why do I need to confront him?"

"So, tell me that you didn't cry when you got home that

night. Tell me that you weren't thinking about it for the past couple of days and that you weren't having a sleepless night." Loris dares Erika.

Erika doesn't reply.

All the emotions she had buried are now coming back.

Loris is right.

She cried a lot that night, and she had trouble sleeping after that. She wants to tell Loris that she's hurting so much. But Loris knows about it already, even if she doesn't tell.

Erika doesn't have to tell her the pain she's feeling. And right now, Erika doesn't trust herself to verbalize what her heart is saying.

She is just feeling everything!

And all these are making her more confused than ever before.

Control yourself, Erika!

Balance!

Remember to balance your heart and your mind.

Erika is talking to herself in her head. It is Erika's attempt not to cry in front of Loris. She tries so hard to compose herself before she speaks again.

"He liked the poem that I gave him as a graduation gift." Erika says.

She is relieved to hear that her voice sounded normal and calm.

"You didn't show me that poem, so I have no idea what it was all about." Loris says.

Erika gets off the bed to get her phone. She opens the file folder and searches for the poem. Shen then hands over the phone to Loris so she can read the poem.

When Loris finishes reading, Erika waits for her to say something. Knowing her, it won't be difficult for Loris to say what's on her mind.

"Love and Reason. I wonder what Anthony's reaction was." Loris says.

She doesn't say much, and Erika is more worried about Loris' lack of words for her.

Erika isn't expecting the question, too.

In her mind, Erika wants an assurance from Loris that her poem doesn't reveal her feelings for Anthony. She wants Loris to tell her that she is safe from this rollercoaster ride Erika feels she's into.

"He said thank you and that he liked it." Erika replies tentatively.

Loris isn't convinced that it was all Anthony said but she doesn't want to press Erika. She just proceeds to ask another question.

"What is the real score between you and Anthony, then?"

"We are friends, Loris! That is the score between us." Erika says.

"Last Tuesday, Anthony looked at you as if he wanted to take you home. He held your hands, walking on the university grounds for all the world to see," says Loris.

Her hands on her hips.

Loris looks like a teacher trying to make a point, Erika thinks.

Loris then continues, "The same as we went out of the restaurant after the graduation dinner. And mind you, his family was all there. So, however much you like to say that you and Anthony are just friends, it didn't change the fact that both of you were acting more than that."

She then added, "Both of you are sizzling with feelings for each other. It showed earlier, too, in Tagaytay. Anthony has only eyes for you. Just for YOU! Do you get me? So, I'm sorry if I don't believe you, Erika!"

Is it true?

Does Anthony look at me like that?

Erika didn't notice because she usually avoids looking directly at Anthony's eyes. She doesn't want Anthony to know how she feels. Her eyes usually give away the emotions she is trying hard to hide.

"What do you want me to say? You already knew that I have feelings for him. It doesn't mean that there's something going on between us."

Erika is getting frustrated by the minute.

She doesn't know what to say anymore.

Why can't they just talk about the financial market or some courtroom cases? Erika feels she has better chances of winning in court arguments than trying to defend what she's feeling or what's going on between her and Anthony.

"We never talk about it. Anthony never mentioned that he has feelings for me. And I don't have any intention of asking him. If you want to know, then go ahead; ask him yourself." Erika says to Loris.

The frustration she's feeling is getting the better of her. Erika's voice sounds as she feels.

"Anthony never said that he loves you because he is exactly like you! You admitted to me that you love him but can't say it to him. He might not be saying it out loud. But I am telling you, Erika, that he loves you." Loris explains.

Loris is trying hard, too, to make Erika see the real big picture between her and Anthony.

"You can't possibly be sure about that! And I can't possibly believe that Anthony loves me, unless he tells me!" Erika replies.

"And besides, even if he loves me, as you keep telling me, it doesn't really matter, don't you think? There's a reason why he is not saying it to me. Anthony has a reason for not pursuing his feelings for me!" Erika continues in frustration.

"OMG Erika. Really? Must Anthony say the words 'I love you' before you feel and know that he loves you? Haven't you noticed how Anthony talks to you and looks at you? They speak volumes!" Loris was trying to convince Erika that Anthony loves her.

"Why is Anthony not telling you? You can ask yourself the same question, Erika. Why are you not telling Anthony that you love him?" Loris added.

Erika has no answer to that, so she just stays quiet and let Loris do the talking.

"Look, Erika. My ex used to say that he loved me. But those are just words! He never looked at me and cared for me the way Anthony is to you. And where is he now? Gone with another one." Loris continues.

Should I believe it?

Should I believe that Anthony loves me more than friends?

Erika's mind is working overtime.

Her heart wants to believe it, but her mind is not one hundred percent sure about it.

OMG!

Think of love and reason, Erika!

Where can I find the balance between my mind and my heart?

It isn't enough.

I need to hear from him that he loves me.

That would be the only way I could be sure about it.

"I can see in your eyes that your brain is trying to form a defense about what I said. It is not a court case, Erika. I simply stated my observations in case you haven't noticed them yourself." Loris says.

It irritates Erika sometimes how transparent she is to Loris. Erika wonders also how Loris can see and read what's inside her head.

"Thank you, Loris," says Erika and means it.

Erika then adds, "I know you want what's best for me. But I must hold on to the fact that Anthony had been in a relationship with Iris and not me. He loved Iris and not me. He might have an affection for me. But that's it. AFFECTION!"

Loris is just listening, but Erika knows that Loris wants to interrupt her. So Erika continues, "I have been dealing with facts every single day. So the fact that Anthony is not saying anything, I will always assume that what he's showing me is just a friendly affection."

"You are afraid. I can see that. I totally understand. But sometimes, in life, we need to take chances." Loris says.

She then continues, "Since you mentioned dealing with facts, isn't it you deal with some risk, too, in business? When you present your financial plan and your analysis of the business trajectories, part of that is some risk."

She looks at Erika with so much understanding. Loris's voice mellows a notch or two also.

But Loris is not finish yet, "Love is not black and white. It isn't a fairy tale either. Sometimes, it's a gamble. Don't be afraid to gamble on love, Erika. If you do, you will just find yourself stuck on your idea of love, and the reality is very different from what you usually imagine."

Erika doesn't dare to say a word after a long litany from Loris.

She understands her best friend's point. Erika wishes she could find in herself the courage to gamble on love.

Love is not just an emotion.

It is not just a matter of the heart.

Love is also a decision.

This is what Erika is thinking all this time.

Soon Erika must decide.

But for now, she just has to feel.

Chapter 14

Anthony is lying on the spare bed in Juris' room.

He'll be staying with Juris and his family the whole weekend. He wants to have more time with Erika before thinking and deciding the way forward. He is supposed to be sleeping by now, but sleep seems to be avoiding him.

Juris is already in deep sleep, but Anthony is very much awake and just staring at the ceiling.

He can still see the flashing **'mylove'** in his mind.

Anthony didn't expect it.

In fact, he didn't know what to expect when he borrowed Erika's phone. He just wants to know.

For what?

Anthony has no idea.

I just want to know. That's it!

Anthony can't forget the look on Erika's face, too. Erika blushed tremendously, as she didn't expect that he would know.

He had this urge to hug her and tell her that it's OK.

I wonder how long my name has been "mylove" on her phone.

He doesn't know what to do, and right now, it feels like he's on a crossroads.

What will I do?

Anthony and his dad had an agreement that if he decides to take up law, Anthony will do it in UL, back home.

His family wants him to come back and spend more time with them, especially now that Anthony's dad is sick.

Love and Reason.

Erika's poem came back to Anthony's mind.

Erika.

Anthony wants to be with Erika, and he is sure of that. After they reconnected, his feelings for her are growing by the minute.

He can't do anything about it, not yet anyway.

Anthony is still in the middle of the crossroads.

He doesn't know what to do.

It would be unfair to Erika if Anthony changed the dynamic of their friendship when he is not yet ready.

But when will you be ready?

Anthony finds himself asking.

Anthony believes that he, himself, has to be ready first and totally committed, without any backlog, before pursuing the feelings he has for Erika.

Erika deserves much more than I could give her right now.

Anthony can see the clock hanging on the wall. He can almost hear the clock ticking: tik-tak-tik-tak!

And every tik and tak of the clock is telling him that he should decide as soon as possible.

Anthony knows that he can't just stay in the middle of this crossroads.

He has to keep going.

For Erika.

For him.

Chapter 15

Erika wakes up before Loris.

She checks the clock on her phone, and it is a little over eight o'clock in the morning. There is a message in her inbox from Anthony. The message came in not so long ago.

Good morning ☺

Anthony is up early.
He is a morning person like her.
Erika types a message.

Good morning to you too! ☺

After sending the text, Erika feels good waking up this morning with a message from Anthony. Erika smiles thinking of him.

Her phone "dings" again for another message.

Can I call you? ☺

Erika looks at Loris and sees that her best friend is still in deep sleep.

She doesn't want to wake Loris up, so she goes out of the bedroom. She goes straight to the kitchen to make herself a cup of coffee with sugar and cream.

Loris' apartment isn't that big, but it is not so small either and very comfortable. Erika is always in Loris's apartment, especially when they were in college.

They used the apartment to hang out, most especially when they had vacant periods in between classes. Erika knows where everything is.

After making her coffee, Erika sits in one of the two chairs in the kitchen. Yes, only two chairs in the kitchen!

Erika then types a one-word reply.

Yup. ☺

And not long after she sends the message, her phone rings.

Erika lets the music go on for a while before she takes up the call.

It is her second time to see the *mylove* flashing on the screen, and she finds herself enjoying the task. It was only yesterday when Erika changed Anthony's name on her phone to *mylove.*

Erika feels she is blushing again after remembering what happened last night.

Now Anthony knew, in a way, her feelings for him.

"Hello!" says Erika.

She sips a few times her coffee and feels that she is already warming up.

"Hey. Good morning. How was your sleep?" Anthony asks her.

Is he always like this in the morning?

Erika wonders.

Even from the other end of the phone, Erika can feel Anthony's energy.

"It was OK. Short but sound, I think," answers Erika.

"Why short?" Anthony asks.

"Loris wanted us to talk. We never had the chance to have this conversation after college. We were busy all the time," explains Erika.

It is a simplified version of what actually transpired between her and her best friend.

"OK. So do you have a plan today? I am thinking about picking you up. We can go to CU. It's been so long since I was there," says Anthony.

Erika thinks about this for a while. Loris didn't mention anything that they will do today.

I guess it is fine.

"No plan for today, I guess. So, yeah, we can go out." Erika answers.

"Awesome! Can I pick you up at around ten? Is that OK?"

"It's fine, I think."

"See you then, Erika! I won't hold you for long, so you can get ready."

"OK. Bye, and see you."

Erika finishes drinking her coffee and goes to the shower. On her way to the bedroom after she showered, Erika notices Loris in the kitchen making herself something to eat.

"Good morning!" Erika greets Loris.

"Good morning to you, too!" Loris answers. She then adds, "You are up so early, I can see."

Erika tells her about Anthony's plan.

Loris smiles and gives Erika a nod.

"Good that Anthony is not wasting any time to have another date with you." Loris teases Erika.

Erika just rolls her eyes and doesn't bother to answer.

Here we go again!

She thinks with a shake of her head.

Erika leaves Loris alone. She doesn't want to be emotional again, most especially not today.

Erika goes to the bedroom to dress up. She's aiming for comfort, so she takes her faded jeans and a summer blouse paired with sandals.

And soon enough, Anthony comes knocking on the door. Loris opens the door and calls Erika. Meanwhile, Anthony and Loris wait for her in the kitchen.

Anthony isn't driving a car when he picks up Erika at Loris' apartment. He commuted. He also just commuted from Manila to Laguna yesterday.

Anthony can tell right away the difference between the air he breathes in Manila and in Laguna.

It's fresher here.

Anthony thinks as he and Erika start walking in the direction of the subdivision gate.

Loris's apartment is located in a subdivision very near CU. Anthony and Erika just walk and take their time.

It is a little cloudy, so it isn't strikingly hot. Although the temperature is still a little over 30 degrees.

He never knew how much he missed Calamba University and Laguna until he comes here today.

As they near the place, Anthony can see the main

building. It is easy to feel this longing for CU because of the castle-like structure.

"I miss this place!" Anthony whispers.

It is Saturday and summer, so the area is quite calm and quiet. There are not many students taking up summer classes.

Erika and Anthony have no trouble going inside the campus. The guards still remember them, and Erika has with her the alumni ID she got not long after she graduated.

They walk to the covered path walk on the way to the main lobby. From there, they can see the chapel and the Mt. Makiling.

"I will never get tired of looking and admiring the view." Anthony says. He is looking over where the mountain is.

"Me too!" Erika replies in agreement.

Anthony holds Erika's hand, and together they walk towards the stage where they had their graduation. Standing there, they have a better view of the open field, the chapel, and the mountain.

Anthony and Erika sit on the stairs, and they observe their surroundings. There are some students playing football on the field.

"I used to play football; you know." Anthony tells Erika.

"Really? But I had never seen you play in college—not even train or something. My goodness, when I think about it, I never even saw you in the football field."

Erika laughs and shakes her head.

"That's because I wasn't that good to play for the varsity team. But I played for the AS Department for two years during intramurals." Anthony clarifies.

Erika's eyes widen in surprise. She can't believe she missed seeing that.

Where was I during those times?

She still couldn't believe it!

"Really? But why didn't I see you then?" Erika asks.

"Well, that I don't know." Anthony says and then smiles at her.

Anthony then continues, "And besides, football wasn't that popular, unlike basketball. So maybe you were watching a basketball game instead of football."

Anthony further explains that he only played when he was in his second and third years.

"I agree with you. Basketball is what we used to watch. I think I had a crush on one of Juris' teammates. I just don't remember his name. All I remember now is that he's from the engineering department."

Erika tells Anthony, and then she laughs at the thought.

Anthony stares at Erika in disbelief.

"Oh, that is new. Definitely! You never told me about that. Seriously? You had a crush on one of the varsity players?" Anthony asks.

"Yes. Why? Is it impossible to think that I am a normal human being? If I am not mistaken, that engineering guy was one of the many crushes I had in college. You can ask Loris." Erika jokes.

It is Anthony's turn to widen his eyes. He shakes his head and stares at her. Really stares at her!

"You are kidding me, right? Tell me now that YOU.ARE.KIDDING.ME," says Anthony.

He is looking straight into Erika's eyes and not even blinking once.

"What? Wait, are you jealous?" Erika asks.

Anthony didn't answer.

He just keeps staring at Erika. He is trying to read the truthfulness of what Erika has just revealed.

Jealous?

YES!

He is jealous!

Maybe I should ask Juris later who the other varsity players on his team during those years were.

Anthony wonders who was that player Erika had fancied before.

Erika waits for Anthony's reply. She never gets any. Instead, Anthony changes their topic back to sports.

"So you played volleyball and chess. Were you a varsity player or just during intramurals, too?" Anthony asks.

But Erika can see that Anthony has other things on his mind.

"Only during intramurals. Like you, I wasn't that good also." Erika admits.

Well, it is true.

"How come you played for two events? Wasn't it difficult? Chess usually had the same schedules as most of the ballgames." Anthony says.

Erika tells Anthony that her first choice was volleyball. But because the AS Department was very much in need of a female chess player, Erika tried out for the team.

They took her to the team. The only agreement was that if the schedules collided with each other, Erika must prioritize chess since it was an individual sport.

Their department during intramurals needed every point they could get.

"I only wanted to play because of the intramural uniform." Erika laughs at the thought, and Anthony is laughing with her.

When their laughter subsides, Erika continues, "I had been paying for the intramural fee every year, and I haven't gotten any T-shirts or souvenirs. Well, that's what I was thinking before."

As they talk more about their college years, Erika begins to fully relax.

She's enjoying every second of it.

I will always treasure this moment when I sit beside Anthony while reminiscing about our past here in CU, the place I will always call my second home.

At quarter to twelve, they stand up from sitting for almost an hour. They walk on the field while they hold their hands towards the university chapel.

They both go inside and pray.

When they are finished, they go outside again and then take some pictures.

Since it is lunchtime already, they both decide to eat. Erika craves crispy chicken and potato mojos, so they agree to have lunch at the nearest pizza parlor near CU. It is not that far so they just take a tricycle to get there.

It is their first time to eat in this place. There wasn't a pizza parlor nearby before, if Erika isn't mistaken. Erika likes the place, though. It doesn't feel crowded.

They find a window seat and sit there. The pizza crew

comes with the menu. Erika and Anthony order the same 'Big Plate of Lunch'.

While they wait for their food, Erika and Anthony simply talk about what they will do after lunch. Anthony asks her if it is OK for them to visit the Rizal Shrine and the 'banga' park again.

Erika is OK with that.

However, Erika has this nagging feeling. She can feel that there's something going on, but she can't pinpoint what it is.

There's more to this than just simply reminiscing. Isn't it?

Their food arrives, and they start eating. They simply talk about different things, lighter topics, and Erika is actually relieved. Right now, she doesn't need heavy stuff. She just wants to enjoy their time together.

After they finish their lunch, they take a jeepney and go to the Rizal Shrine. Many local tourists are already inside when they come. Erika and Anthony had seen most of the things inside the house before.

But this fact doesn't stop them from enjoying their visit, as if they hadn't been there before at all.

Erika's heart is drumming so hard.

There's a strong emotion flooding her heart and coursing through her brain. And she can't shake this feeling out of her system. She can't explain it either.

When they reach the 'wishing well' part, Anthony took out two 10-peso coins from his pocket.

He gives one to Erika and says, "Remember what we used to do during our visits here? When we weren't busy, we used to talk over here. And when we do have coins, we throw them and make a wish."

Anthony is looking at Erika earnestly as he speaks.

It's all coming back to her.

Those days.

The start of their friendship.

And now Anthony is reminding her of those times.

Erika is getting more emotional. Her tears are threatening to drop any time soon. Erika turns to wipe the tears from her eyes.

"Hey, what's wrong?" Erika hears Anthony ask her.

She tries to compose herself before answering.

"Nothing. I think I caught something in my eyes." Erika tries not to confess.

She doesn't want to show Anthony how weak she is right now. Erika can't deal with her vulnerable side at that moment.

"Let me see it," offers Anthony.

"No! I'm OK now. It's no big deal."

Erika turns toward Anthony again and smiles. "So, wish. Let's make a wish. You first."

Anthony doesn't say a thing.

He just stares at Erika.

He studies her face while trying not to grab and hug her. Anthony is sure that Erika cried. He can still see it in her eyes. There is sadness in her eyes even if she's smiling.

When Erika said that she's OK, he wanted to call her on it. He controlled himself. Anthony knew that Erika is a proud woman. She doesn't want to show her emotion most of the time.

Erika's toughness is what he admires the most, especially when they were in college. And Anthony can still see that toughness in her right now.

"OK. Let me think first of what I will wish this time," Anthony says, and then he smiles so brightly at Erika.

"You really come prepared with the coins!" Erika says with a smile. This time, her smile reaches her eyes.

"Was it obvious?" Anthony asks.

He then laughs.

"Not so!" Erika laughs, too.

Anthony then closes his eyes, and when he opens them, it doesn't take long before he casts the coin in the well.

My stay is nearing the end again, and Erika has shown me the road I want to take. I hope and wish that this road will lead me back to her one day!

This is what is inside Anthony's head. He realizes that he's been wishing it for a long time.

Anthony turns and smiles at Erika.

"I guess it's now your turn to make a wish," he says.

Erika smiles and turns toward the wishing well. Erika then closes her eyes, not to make a wish but to pray.

Lord, I don't know where fate will lead us. Please guide me and Anthony as we travel the path towards our own dream, and the happiness we both desire. I don't know if this will be the last time we will be together, but I pray and hope that the friendship we have built over the years will last. Amen.

When Erika opens her eyes, she looks at Anthony and notices that Anthony is staring at her.

And before Erika can say something, Anthony reaches for her and hugs her. Erika then hears Anthony say, "I do hope our wishes will come true."

After Anthony and Erika made their wishes, they walked towards the small 'Bahay kubo' or Nipa hut located in the yard outside the house facing St. John the Baptist church.

"I decided to pursue my dream. I will study law this coming semester," Anthony says to Erika as they sit on the vacant bench they see near the hut.

"Wow! That's good," Erika says, and she means it.

But Erika hears the sadness in his voice, so she asks, "Why do you seem sad?"

"I got mixed emotions about it. Don't get me wrong. I want to study law, and I guess it has always been my dream to become a lawyer." Anthony says.

He looks at her as if waiting for Erika to say something. When Erika says not a single word, Anthony just continues. "I promised my dad that I will study law at UL."

Studying law at UL.

Erika feels she just has rooted to the spot.

Her brain is racing so fast about what can possibly happen from now on. Her emotions are swirling, and she's unable to control the pain that suddenly comes anew.

You have recently come back into my life, and now you are leaving again.

This is what Erika wants to say. But she can't and won't. She is not in the position to say that.

It is definitely not Anthony's fault that I am feeling this way. I can't hold him back from his dreams. He's been supporting me all these years. The only thing I can do for him now is to give him the same support he deserves.

This is what Erika's mind has been thinking about, and yet her heart is crying.

Erika is suddenly lost for words.

She wants to say something, but it feels like she's holding back for whatever reason unknown to her.

Everything is just in her head, and the words can't find their way out.

"Aren't you going to say something?" Anthony asks.

He sees that Erika is very quiet for quite a while.

Anthony's voice is like medicine that makes Erika mobile again.

"If that is what you really want, I am happy for your choice," Erika says.

Her voice is very low. It sounds like a whisper already.

How about us?

She wants to ask.

Us?

Really, Erika?

There's no you and him!

And Erika knows that there's really no 'us' between them, especially now that Anthony is leaving her again.

Anthony looks at Erika and studies her face. Erika is on the verge of crying. Her tears are threatening to fall.

The worst part is that it's all my fault.

Anthony's brain is telling him.

He doesn't want to see Erika like this. He hates himself for making Erika so sad. It's almost unbearable for Anthony.

And right on cue, someone comes to where they are sitting and asks Anthony if he can take their picture. He says to give him a second. He doesn't want to be rude to the person, but Anthony wants to make sure that Erika is OK.

Erika looks at Anthony and says, "I'm OK. Go help them." Anthony sees Erika smile; he is relieved.

She's regaining her control.

That's what Anthony is thinking.

He then goes to the family who wants their picture taken.

Sitting on the bench alone, Erika is counting one to ten in her head. The counting helps Erika calm herself. She's been doing it since she can remember.

It works every time for her.

She is thankful for the temporary distraction.

Erika almost cried in front of Anthony. The look on his face said it all. Anthony is blaming himself, and Erika knows that. And that's not right. Erika won't be able to forgive herself if Anthony keeps blaming himself for making her cry.

The Erika she knows is a strong woman.

And right now, Anthony needs that woman.

I will not cry in front of him.

My tears can wait until I come home.

It is three o'clock when Anthony and Erika decide to leave the shrine. They walk towards the 'banga' park for a quick visit and take pictures. They go up in the banga and take their picture there, too.

After a couple of shots, they go down and walk towards St. John the Baptist Church. They go inside. Anthony holds Erika's hand as they both kneel and pray.

This calm them both.

Anthony takes Erika home in Los Baños. The silence between them is so deafening. But her body, heart, and mind are so tired right now that she just let it be.

Anthony stays for a while at Erika's house.

They sit on a wooden chair outside. Erika has a little garden in their yard, which her mother is maintaining. It's Erika's favorite place. Here, Erika can relax.

Anthony is drinking a cup of black coffee, while Erika is having warm green tea. After a sip of her tea, Erika asks, "When are you coming back to Legazpi?"

Her voice is now back to normal.

"Last week of July. I will just finish all my backlogs at work and prepare for a transition. I will also process my papers at the university so all the documents I needed for law school are ready." Anthony replies.

"It's happening so fast. You are like a whirlwind in my boring life!" Erika says jokingly.

They both laugh.

From the outside, everything seems OK, but in Erika's heart and mind, there's a storm currently brewing.

"But it won't be the last time we will see each other, Erika. I will come here before I go back to Legazpi," says Anthony.

They talk for more than an hour. The sky is clear now unlike earlier. They can see some stars from where they are seated.

"Can you see that constellation?" Anthony points to Erika stars pattern in the sky.

He explains to her the different point to it to distinguish

it from the others. "The brightest of them all, in that constellation is called *Regulus*."

"What is the name of that constellation?" Erika asks.

"Leo." Anthony answers.

"It is your constellation. You are Leo!" Erika exclaims.

"Yes. And every time you will look at it, I hope that you'll remember me. And know that we are looking at it together," says Anthony solemnly.

Around six in the evening, Anthony says his goodbye to Erika's mother, but not to her.

Anthony has never said goodbye to her.

As in never!

Erika doesn't remember the last time he has ever said goodbye.

It's always *'See you when I see you'* or *'until next time'*.

Before going out of the gate, Anthony hugs Erika. He wants Erika to feel all his emotions in that hug. He can't say anything he wants to say—nothing at all.

Anthony just lets his hug do the talking.

He doesn't know how long he holds Erika in his arms. Anthony just knows that it isn't enough.

Chapter 16

In the stillness of time
Our friendship goes a mile
Clouds above our sky
And the gray between us!

When Anthony left, Erika went to her room and cried.

She lets all the tears fall.

She is letting out all her unspoken emotions. Erika is thankful that she was able to control her tears earlier.

Erika has too many questions to ask Anthony, but she couldn't ask him.

And now, here she is, alone in her room, with a broken heart.

Loving him doesn't mean he has to love me, too.

Erika tried to reason it out.

Aside from mending her heart, the only thing she can do, and always did, is reason out.

Anthony didn't ask her to love him, and she didn't say it to him either.

With a confused mind and a broken heart, Erika whispers, "*I would just love him from afar then.*"

It's nearly three in the morning, and Erika is still awake. Her tears had dried up, and she is now calm.

But her mind is still processing everything.

Love is not just an emotion and not just a matter of the heart.

It has always been Erika's mantra.

It doesn't mean she is not hurting and doesn't mean she will stop loving.

It only means that in the end, she will decide whether

it's time to let go.

This feeling will be in her heart, but it will not cage her in her life.

Instead of just lying in bed, Erika sits up and takes her notebook and pen from the side table.

She will scribble her thoughts and feelings.

Since it's hard for her to verbalize what she feels for Anthony, Erika will use her pen to express them.

And when the time comes, she will give it to Anthony.

After nearly two hours, Erika is only able to write a poem with two stanzas with four lines each.

Your embrace said it all
It is time for us to move on
Though crying is not easy
Tears coming down so freely

Too many unspoken words
In our own created world
It is like a bubble of dreams
Can you hear my heart scream?

Erika sighs.

She can feel the tiredness creeping in. She stops writing and turns off the lights.

I will just continue tomorrow.

Maybe tomorrow, everything will be OK.

Just a maybe.

She then proceeds to the bed and lays there until finally

sleep takes over.

It is after lunch when Erika finally wakes up the following day. She feels less awful than before Erika fell asleep. She is hungry, too.

Erika goes out of her room to eat lunch and drink coffee with cream and sugar. Erika badly needs the caffeine to fully wake her up.

When she is done eating lunch and drinking coffee, she showers.

It's Sunday, and Erika will attend the Sunday mass with her mom.

Erika and her mother usually attend afternoon Sunday mass at the Immaculate Conception Parish Church in Los Baños. But for the past year, Erika wasn't able to do so because she was in Manila during weekends attending classes in TLS.

As she is dressing up, Erika notices the poem she is trying to write last night, or rather very early today. She is hoping that she will be able to finish it later this evening when they get back.

Inside the church, during the homily, Erika can't concentrate. Her mind is busy with something else, so she asks God for forgiveness.

However, Erika can't control where her mind and heart travel.

My heart is beginning to say something.
Is this what I really want?
Is this who I am?
Am I too emotional?
No.
Erika doesn't think so.

She is just beginning to dwell deeper on herself.

What Erika feels and thinks affects her whole being. She doesn't know if she's making sense, and Erika doesn't care at all.

She just wants to express herself.

In her many years of existence, Erika has learned to keep her feelings to herself.

Erika thinks it is okay for her to be 'just friends' with Anthony.

Is this really what she feels?

Somehow, Erika feels the emptiness inside. And she doesn't like it.

How could I ever let it be?

Loris told Erika that she's insane and that Erika is a martyr. But Erika doesn't think so.

She prefers to call it 'true love'.

When Erika realized that she's in love with Anthony, she never expected him to love her too. Erika just accepted and embraced the feeling. They texted each other and sent messages via email. Sometimes, when time permitted, they called each other.

Their friendship and Erika's love for Anthony grew bigger than she expected.

And when Anthony told Erika that he would be leaving again to pursue his dream, she just let her feelings consume her.

She is pursuing her dream; why can't Anthony do the same?

That's what Erika's mind is telling her.

Erika may be crying from the inside, but she has to be

tough outside. It's already difficult for her; Erika doesn't want Anthony to feel the same.

She appreciates the fact that Anthony is sharing his plans and dreams with her.

And maybe that is enough!

Instead of going back home, after the Sunday mass, Erika and her mother go to a restaurant near them to eat dinner.

This restaurant serves both Filipino and Korean cuisines. Erika's mother likes pork sinigang (a sour soup with pork and vegetables, and the broth is tamarind-flavored) and oil-fried boneless *bangus* or milkfish with fried garlic bits on top, so she treats her mother to dinner.

Back at home, Erika goes straight to her room.

She rests for a while.

Erika doesn't remember the last time she ate too much to the point of feeling so bloated.

As Erika lays in her bed, she sees again her notebook on top of her side table.

She then remembers the poem isn't finished yet.

She stands up and gets the notebook.

Erika reads the two stanzas she was able to write last night. After a while, all the emotions keep coming back.

Both her mind and heart are in full force, and Erika doesn't know which one she will listen to.

Erika's mind is telling her something that her heart is not willing to accept.

After a couple of hours, she is finally finished with the poem.

Should I email this poem to Anthony right now?

Or should I give it to him before he travels back to

Legazpi?

For someone who wants to be a lawyer, Erika is always torn about what she will do when it comes to her heart and to Anthony.

Anthony is definitely my Kryptonite.

Erika smiles.

It would be exciting to know what will happen when I meet him in the courtroom one day and we sit on the opposite side.

Erika opens her laptop and decides to email the poem to Anthony.

She has to be brave.

As Loris said to her, Erika should start taking her chance.

She types the poem in the email itself instead of having it as an attachment.

Subject: Poem (just borrowing the subject from your last email)

Anthony,

I am sending this poem to you. I can't think of the title yet. So, bear with me!

<No title yet>

Looking at the sky above us
While reminiscing about the past
Those times spent together

Will be in our hearts forever

Your embrace said it all
It is time for us to move on
Though crying is not easy
Tears coming down so freely

Too many unspoken words
In our own created world
It is like a bubble of dreams
Can you hear my heart scream?

Heading in a different direction
Confused about mixed emotion
Is true love only an illusion?
Or you and I an exception?

This feeling of uncertainty
A silent promise without security
Afraid to lose a part of me
And be alone on this journey

Will I know again this kind of love?
Can I replace you in my heart?
Questions linger in my mind
I hope one day answers I can find

I wish you luck in your new journey. I will be looking at 'Leo' from now on.

Erika

She reads the poem a couple of times. She stares at the send button but can't quite click it yet.

She is sorting everything inside her head.

As a financial analyst, Erika is so familiar with the process of determining all the risk factors involved in each given situation.

And right now, Erika is doing the same; the risks, rewards, and even some contradictions of sending the poem to Anthony are being processed and factored in her head.

The analyst in her is temporarily taking over. Erika's mind is in overtime mode.

But however organized she is in almost all aspects of her life, Erika still finds herself in the middle of chaos and a mess. She is just hoping that it will not be forever like this.

Erika prays that it is just a rare occurrence.

And somehow, the analyst in her continues.

It is now time for Erika to hear from her inner resonance. She needs to prioritize everything based on their importance in her life.

Maybe, and it is just a maybe, Erika can find the calmness in her to deal with the chaotic emotions she's feeling right now.

Erika takes a deep breath and then counts from one to ten before she finally clicks send.

Now, I have done it!

She just has to wait for Anthony's reaction.

Chapter 17

Two months later...

It is the last Friday of July that year when Erika receives a text message from Anthony. Erika is having lunch with her colleagues in the company canteen.

> Hi. I am in Laguna right now. Can we meet? When do you finish your shift? ☺

Erika forgets that July is almost over. She is busy lately catching up with work. She has also been traveling back and forth to Manila to process her new semester in TLS.

Erika had been to a popular bookstore in Morayta, Manila, with Loris, to buy her new sets of textbooks. Her mind is so full of job- and school-related stuff that Erika forgets that they are nearing the end of the month.

> Hey. Really? I will be finished at 4pm.

Erika clicks send and waits for a reply. Soon after, the message comes in.

> Great! I can borrow Juris' car to pick you up at work. ☺

Oh, no. I need time to prepare myself.

Erika's mind works quickly after reading Anthony's reply.

There's no need. I'll take the company shuttle bus. We can meet at SM Crossing.

Why do I always sound so formal, even in text messages? Erika doesn't understand herself either.

Shuttle bus?

Really, Erika?

It's a lame excuse!

Sometimes, Erika is irritated at herself.

Why does she need to be in control every time?

Can't she lose herself once in a while?

Ding!

A reply from Anthony.

OK. Just message me when you get there. I will just be roaming around while waiting. ☺

Anthony is in Laguna.

Erika can't concentrate at work thinking about it, about him.

Luckily, Erika has finished all the reports her boss needs next week. She is just reviewing them to double check, and now she is also almost done with the reviews.

Good for her, though, because her mind right now is

very much occupied with Anthony.

How time flies!

It seems just like yesterday when Anthony told Erika about his plan. She remembers that Anthony said he would see Erika before going back to Legazpi.

What happened with those two months?

Until now, she's not getting any reply from Anthony about the poem she sent him.

There was silence between them for those two months.

But Erika doesn't want to annoy Anthony by sending him text messages often, so she has just been patiently waiting for him to call or text her the whole time.

Although Erika wants to know what Anthony thinks about the poem she sent him, she doesn't send any message at all.

Has Anthony received my poem?

Has he opened it?

The only message Anthony sent her the past two months was another poem. But he didn't mention anything about the poems Erika sent him.

Erika looks at her phone and opens her email.

She is thankful that the technology now is much more advanced than when she was in university. She only needs her phone to compose and send an email message, unlike before, when she needed her laptop every time.

Erika scrolls her phone a few times to find the poem Anthony sent her. When she finds it, she reads it again.

One summer night

As I sit on a wooden chair
Just outside of where I stay
I looked up at the sky above
And I uttered a little prayer

As the wind touches my skin
It blows a whisper into my ears
Sending a simple message
And your name is all I heard

As the moon and stars shine
Their light reflects on my eyes
My body feels the summer chill
Making all my emotions swirl

As the night started to unfold
And our own story is being told
A story with a beautiful beginning
It's a short story without an ending!

Erika was with Loris when she received Anthony's email message. They were in Morayta, Manila.

She now realizes that she didn't reply to him.

Not that day.

Not even until now.

And as she reads again the poem, she can picture their story being told and how beautiful the beginning of that story is.

And Erika agrees.

Their story, however beautiful the beginning was, is still short and has no ending yet.

It is almost five o'clock when Erika finally reaches SM in Calamba. She sends a message to Anthony saying that she will be entering via the mall entrance near a pizza restaurant.

Erika enters the mall, and she sees Anthony right away. He's sitting on a chair outside a coffee shop.

Anthony smiles as Erika approaches him.

"Hi," says Erika.

"Hello," replies Anthony.

He greets her with a kiss on her cheek.

Erika blushes, and she smiles to cover it.

"Are you hungry? Where do you want to eat?" asks Anthony.

"I'm not hungry yet. What about you?"

"A little. I want to eat where we could also talk." Anthony says. He then continues, "I also want to relax. I worked so hard the last two months that I think my body needs the natural hot springs that come from the mountain. I want to swim."

"Do you have the things you need to go for a swim?" Erika asks.

"I actually bought them while waiting for you," says Anthony, and then he grins.

"An expensive night swim it seems!" teases Erika.

Erika has no plan of buying anything. She will get her things at home.

She calls Loris and explains to her their plan this evening. Erika then asks Loris if she can sleepover tonight in the apartment. She keeps some things at Loris.

In fact, Erika's things from her last sleepover were still at Loris.

After Loris agrees, Erika then calls her mother.

Anthony and Erika then commute to get some of her things for swimming in their house.

The restaurant and the resort Erika and Anthony will go to are not that far from where Erika lives. So, after packing her things she needs, Erika and Anthony walk out of the house.

Anthony says goodbye to her mother, and he makes a promise that he will see to it that Erika comes safe at Loris' tonight.

They walk out of the subdivision and cross the street. They walk a little further to the right in the direction of Calamba, and soon after they are in front of the restaurant.

There are only a few people inside when Erika and Anthony come. The waiter directs them to a table for two beside the window, overlooking the highway.

When they both settle on their seats, the waiter takes their order. Erika orders *Your Solo Plate* with lechon kawali, plain white rice, steam vegetables, and fresh ubod spring rolls.

Anthony, on the other hand, orders the *Our Chef's Plate* solo meal, which has a quarter of grilled chicken, rice, pancit canton, steamed vegetables, and deep-fried spring rolls.

As they wait for their meals to come, they talk about different things that are safe and neutral. No one of them mentions law school, poems, or anything about relationships.

And all the while, Erika is searching for her feelings.

At the back of her mind, she's assessing their situation. Anthony may not be disclosing his feelings, but Erika knows and feels that she is important to him.

At the end of the day, Anthony values whatever they

have between them. The fact that he's here with her is a testimony that whatever it is between them is something special to him.

Their meals arrive, and Erika and Anthony start to eat. And while eating, Erika can feel the vast amount of emotion she has for Anthony coursing through her.

Looking at Anthony opposite her, Erika's heart rejoices.

Always be thankful for every opportunity.

This is what her mother used to tell Erika.

"Taste is like beauty, you know. It is not definite, but rather relative," says Anthony.

What?

Taste?

What taste?

Beauty? Huh?!

Erika is freaking out!

She is not sure if she heard Anthony right.

OMG!

I am drifting again.

Definite?

Relative?

Wait! Are we talking about relativity now?

She was so immersed in her own thoughts that she didn't focus on what they were discussing.

Anthony notice that Erika isn't replying. She seems lost in the conversation.

"Erika?"

He turns serious and asks, "Do you have questions you want to ask me?"

This is when Anthony notices Erika's mini trance.

Erika comes to her senses upon hearing the question from Anthony.

Do I have to ask him?

YES!

However, she doesn't know how.

There are too many questions to ask. There are many gray areas between them that Erika thinks need clearing.

Erika wants to ask about Iris.

She also wants to know about Anthony's reaction to her poem.

What will happen to us?

Have you ever loved me?

Or maybe she can ask Anthony if he just always sees her as a friend and nothing more.

But she couldn't do it!

She's chickening out again!

"When are you going back to Legazpi?" Erika finally asks.

Lame! Erika, so lame!

"Tomorrow is my flight," replies Anthony.

He's staring at me again.

Wait?

What?

His flight is tomorrow!

"Tomorrow? But why are you here?" asks Erika.

What about me?

Erika wants to ask.

"I want to spend my last night here with you," replies Anthony. "I don't know when we will meet again."

OMG!

It burns in her heart.

Erika can't breathe for a moment.

She is hyperventilating.

Anthony is leaving tomorrow!

Tomorrow!

He is leaving me!

Erika is motionless.

She can't do it.

She can't find her wit. Only now that the full force of the situation is sinking into her.

What will I do?

OMG!

Erika can feel the tears forming in her eyes. But she needs to get her head together.

I will not cry!

Not now, not here.

Not in front of him!

Oh please, Lord, help me!

"What's wrong? Erika, look at me." Anthony asks.

He has an idea of what's happening. Erika is losing control.

His Erika.

The woman he admires, respects, and loves all these years is losing control of her emotions.

It is not often.

Anthony reaches for Erika's hand. He wants Erika to feel that it's OK, that no matter what happens, nothing will ever change.

Although he doesn't want to give her a promise now.

He wants Erika to be free.

He wants to be free. Only then can they be both happy. They have to fulfill their dreams first, and one day, if heaven's willing, this love between them can go the distance.

Yes. I know I love her.

Anthony asks the waiter for their bill.

He thinks it's better for Erika to be out of the restaurant and breathe some fresh air. It will help her regain her control.

And since the resort is just a few meters away from the restaurant, Erika and Anthony walk there.

And all the while, Anthony is holding Erika's hand.

He is right.

The moment they reach the lobby of the resort, Erika is almost back to her old self.

Anthony pays for a day tour, which is up to 10 p.m. at the reception. They will not take long.

Anthony just wants to swim and relax after months of stress from his studies and work.

His emotional turmoil of wanting to tell Erika his feelings for her, but he couldn't say it, is leaving him sleepless almost every night.

The imbalance between his mind and heart is taking a toll on him.

Anthony hopes that the natural, hot spring water from Mt. Makiling can help his body and mind relax.

The water from this inactive volcano is good for the body because it is enriched with minerals that boost blood circulation and relieve pain.

This is according to local folks here and, of course, based on some research studies of the mountain.

Right now, Anthony badly needs the energy the mountain can provide.

Most of all, he wants to spend the last few hours they have together. He needs to be with Erika.

"Aren't you going to swim yet?" Anthony asks.

Anthony has been swimming back and forth in the big hourglass-shaped swimming pool for quite a while now.

There are only a few people swimming there. Anthony guesses that some resort guests are having their dinner on the restaurant side of the resort, some are inside their rooms already, and some are in the other swimming pools.

The resort is big and clean, and it has many swimming pools. They also have energy pools with different temperatures ranging from 37 to 43 degrees.

Anthony plans on trying that energy pool, but for now he will keep on swimming.

"Later. I am just going to watch you swim," replies Erika.

Erika finds watching Anthony swim back and forth is fun. But the truth of the matter is that Erika doesn't know how to swim.

She is just sitting on the side of the pool while her feet are dangling in the water.

Anthony smiles, and he continues to swim away from her.

Erika watches Anthony swim and sometimes floats in the water.

Erika is thinking how happy she is to love him.

Yes.

I love him!

Erika knows that she can't have him, most especially now. She loves him still, even if Erika is not sure if the love is reciprocal.

And even if her love is reciprocated, Erika is not sure if Anthony loves her the way she loves him.

And right now, there are too many gray areas between us.

Erika tries to find in her the power to be happy despite the circumstances between them.

She is thankful and glad for this moment.

Earlier in the restaurant, she had a temporary break down. Erika will try not to have a repeat of that.

She will only think of happy thoughts from now on.

Erika looks at the sky and smiles.

Only the moon and the stars are gracing the sky tonight, whispers Erika.

Once in a while, Anthony will look in her direction and smile. Erika will look back at him and smile at him, too.

And as she watches Anthony float in the water, facing directly into the sky, Erika utters a little prayer.

Lord, you know my heart's desire and what I truly feel for Anthony. I don't have the courage to say it out loud to Anthony right now, especially that he will be leaving to chase his own dream as I chase mine. But I humbly ask Your divine mercy, Oh Lord, to continue to guide him. And may Anthony be happy wherever fate takes him. Anthony and I may not be meant to be together for now, but I do hope and pray that one day we can be together. That our paths will cross again. But if that day does not come and You have a better plan for both of us, I pray that nothing will ever change and that Anthony and I will be forever friends. I am forever grateful to You, Oh Lord. Amen.

After twenty minutes of swimming back and forth, Anthony swims towards where Erika is sitting.

He smiles and says, "The water is good. Are you just going to sit there all night?"

Anthony teases Erika.

"Of course not! I am just enjoying watching the moon and the stars. I am trying to find Leo, too," answers Erika.

Anthony sits beside her and helps her finding the constellation he pointed at her last time.

They can clearly see the stars as the lights in the resort are all mellows.

They both enjoy the little star gazing episode they have. When they're done, Anthony encourages Erika to swim.

"OK. But I have to warn you that I don't know how to swim. So, it won't really like swimming for me. It's more of dipping." Erika laughs.

"No worries. I can teach you how to swim," says Anthony and winks at her.

And Anthony does that.

He teaches Erika how to swim.

Erika is saving all these in her brain's memory bank.

It is quarter to ten in the evening when Erika and Anthony finally walk out of the resort.

They cross the street while holding hands.

As they wait for a jeepney, Anthony says, "Thank you for being with me."

Erika smiles. She doesn't reply.

"It means a lot to me, Erika," continues Anthony, as he stares at Erika as if trying to memorize her face.

Erika begins to feel conscious; therefore, she just asks Anthony about the poem she sent him two months ago.

"Have you read the poem I sent you?" Erika asks.

But before Anthony can answer, a jeep going to Crossing Calamba stops in front of them.

They go inside, and Anthony pays the driver their fare.

Anthony and Erika are both quiet as the jeepney travels. Both seem occupied by their own thoughts. They go off the jeep when it stops in the corner street going to Loris' subdivision.

Even if there are still tricycles in the area, Anthony says to Erika that he wants to walk instead.

Erika thinks that Anthony wants to prolong their time together. That is what Erika wants, too.

Anthony holds her hand again as they walk along the street.

"Yes," says Anthony.

"Yes?" asks Erika. Confused.

"You asked me earlier if I have read your poem; the answer is yes," explains Anthony.

He then continues, "But it was not after a month you sent it. I was so busy that I didn't open my email."

Erika didn't say anything.

She just stares at Anthony and waits for him to say more.

In her mind, Erika is preparing herself for whatever it is that Anthony will say next.

But he didn't say more.

Anthony and Erika continue to walk slowly, and they only stop upon reaching the front side of the campus, just outside.

Anthony faces the main building and says, "I won't be able to forget this place. I have a lot of memories from here."

"You can always visit if you want to," says Erika.

Anthony turns his head towards Erika and smiles at her. He then says, "After I read your poem, I was more conflicted than ever before. I was so happy and sad at the same time. What you wrote was exactly what I was feeling, and it sealed the feelings I have for you, especially after spending the day with you, Erika."

He pauses for a while and looks directly into Erika's eyes before he continues, "And every time I read a poem from you, it feels like it is my own poem—a poem that I wrote just for you. It always blows my mind how you can write something that I myself am thinking of saying."

His confession goes deep in Erika's heart.

Anthony has feelings for me, too.

Anthony's confession is enough for Erika to be glad.

Erika can't control everything in her life. She can just accept the things she can't change. Knowing that Anthony feels the same way for her is way more than enough.

Erika cannot ask for more.

She is happy that she knows how to love, and Erika allows that love to grow. Even if that love accompanies the hurt she is feeling sometimes, it doesn't matter now because what is important is she knows how to love.

Erika knows that every painful and complicated

experience will only give her hope and strength for the coming days. And she will live to fight for another day.

Love is not just an emotion.

It is not just a matter of the heart. For love is far more complex than that.

"I will miss this place, just like before," says Anthony.

Anthony looks up at the sky and reminisces those times when he was still studying in that campus. He tells Erika that he will miss his alma mater.

As Anthony looks back at the main building, Erika takes the opportunity to study Anthony's face. She is memorizing every perfection and flaw of it.

Thank you, Lord, for this opportunity to be with him for the last time.

"Thank you for asking me out tonight and for spending the time with me before you leave," says Erika.

Anthony didn't say a thing.

He just gets an envelope in his pocket and gives it to Erika. When Erika takes the envelope, Anthony says, "My flight is at seven in the morning. I want you to promise me that you will open the envelop around that time."

"Why?" asks Erika.

"So, I can picture you reading what's inside while I am airborne. At the same time, you can picture me saying to you all the words that are written there," answers Anthony.

"In that sense, it will still feel that we are together."

Anthony smiles.

He is still holding Erika's hand. He doesn't let go of her hand.

He doesn't want to let her go.

And then Anthony hugs her and says, “I will miss you, Erika.”

But the way he hugs Erika is like telling her more than what he can say at that moment.

With tears in her eyes, Erika hugs him back and says, “I will miss you, too!”

Chapter 18

Six years later…

My dear Erika,

I have never imagined that I will be leaving again. Especially when we just recently reconnected after a long time. My decision to study law doesn't come just out of the blue. I've been toying with the idea for as long as I can remember.

Every single time that I talked to you inspired me to follow this dream. Your enthusiasm and dedication grew on me. And all these times, I am also thinking about you and the feelings I have for you.

I am torn between following my dream and staying to give 'Us' a chance. But I want to be ready and able to give my all, my 100%, to you, and that will only happen if there's no backlog on my part.
That is why, when you gave me the poem 'Love and Reason', I stayed awake that night. I was really conflicted. I was trying to find the balance between my mind and my heart. Only you can make me feel and act this way. And I am saying this as a compliment.

Do you remember the poem I wrote back in Legazpi, or at least the last part of it?

As my stay nears the end
The moon above lights my way
I can clearly see the road I'll take
I hope it leads me to you one day

I wrote that poem thinking of you. Until now, I still feel the same way for you. I am hoping that the road I am taking will someday lead me to you, Erika.

As I am writing this letter, I have read your last poem over and over again. I can feel every word you have written. I can't promise anything right now. I want us to be free. It will be unfair for us both if we will be holding on to promises that we don't really know if we can ever fulfill.

I have many questions in my mind too, like you do. And I am hoping that one day I will also find the answers to all those questions.

One thing I can say without a doubt though is that I love you, Erika. I always am and always will. I don't want to analyze the kind of love I have for you. I just want to feel it in my heart.

As you soar high trying to reach the sky, always remember that you are not alone. I am flying with you. Like the poem I wrote for 'Us', we can soar together in the sky.

Soaring Together

With my wings spread so wide
I can soar high up above the sky
But I will be so lonely on my own
It's better if you can come along

Together, we can dance with the wind
Play with the clouds beneath our wings
Let us fly side by side with each other
Towards the direction we remember

We can fly over the mountain skyline
Do it again and again to last a lifetime
We can reach the stars and the moon
It doesn't matter how far or how soon

When it's time for us to come back
And our adrenaline has worn out
We can always remember this time
We soared high together in the sky

I will miss you, Erika.

With much love,
Anthony

P.S.

It is not a goodbye, but it will always be until next time.

For the nth time, Erika reads the last letter she had received from Anthony. The one that Anthony gave her before leaving.

And as promised, she read the letter for the first time at around fifteen minutes past seven o'clock in the morning.

That was after she got a message from Anthony that he's already on the plane and soon he would turn off his phone.

And now, she's reading it again.

Erika is sitting on her condominium in Makati, reading the letter and the poem while having a cup of tea.

It was a tiring day for her.

And an adventurous one!

She was out with Loris. They went to Dapitan arcade because Loris would buy something for her apartment.

Erika smiles as she remembers what happened earlier that day.

"Can you walk slowly? Why are you such in a hurry?!" Erika asked Loris as she tried to catch up to her.

They were walking around Dapitan arcade.

It is December, and the whole country is already in full swing in preparation for the upcoming Christmas.

Loris asked Erika three days ago if she could accompany Loris in buying some decorations and gifts.

Since Erika is free and not traveling back to Laguna that day, she agreed.

It's not that far from her condominium anyway.

Three years ago, Erika quit her job in Laguna after she received a job offer as a senior financial analyst in a leading BPO company in the Philippines.

She then moved to Makati City as her new job provides free-living accommodation there.

Since law school demanded much time from her, it was a better choice.

Accepting the job and moving closer to the TLS campus paid off. A year after, Erika graduated from law school. She took the bar exam and passed.

Now, Erika is a full-pledge lawyer in the same BPO company where she is working and a member of Association of Lawyers in the Philippines.

They offered her a position she couldn't refuse.

Last year, Loris also left Laguna and started working in a government institution in Quezon City, while teaching part-time in one of the colleges nearby.

"Well, we need to hurry up before many other folks come, and it will be difficult to roam around," said Loris.

It was Erika's first time to come to Dapitan arcade. She heard of the place before; actually, many she knew used to come and shop in this arcade. But only now Erika is able to visit the place.

Thanks to Loris.

Dapitan arcade offers a variety of home and Christmas decorations, different crafts and craft supplies, and much more. And since Christmas is near, the arcade was full of vibrant and glittering colors all around.

Erika felt the full uniqueness of the shopping experience.

"How can you find something to buy if you will not slow down or stop, and look around?" Erika asked.

And she meant it.

Sometimes Erika wonders how Loris is able to find and buy something when she walks so fast and hops from one store to another. She didn't only mean in Dapitan arcade but in almost all shopping malls and local markets Erika and Loris went to before.

It is so insane!

Erika kept looking left and right, as the place was new to her. There were many things to see, and many products to choose from. She had, in fact, difficulty focusing on one.

"Why did you stop?" Loris asked Erika.

Erika was holding a small, vibrant-colored hanging lamp with a beautiful flower design that she thought her mother would like.

She showed it to Loris.

"I think mom will like it. I can give it to her next week," replied Erika.

Erika asked the woman in the counter how much the lamp was. After they agreed on the price, Erika bought the lamp.

They continued their store hopping.

As they turned left after they passed through the shop that sells vases and pots, Loris asked, "Is that Anthony?"

Erika looked at the guy Loris was pointing at.

The guy was standing in front of the Christmas lantern store and wearing a white t-shirt, a beige-colored men's short, and a white canvas sneaker. He had very black, shiny hair.

Although the guy has his back at them, Erika still

recognized him.

Anthony!

Erika was sure of that.

Although she couldn't see his face.

"Come on, Erika! Let's go and talk to him," said Loris, and she started walking.

Erika followed her after.

They were careful not to bump anyone.

But since there were many shoppers in the area, it took Erika and Loris a while before they were able to reach the place where they saw Anthony.

But he was not there anymore.

Erika's head turned left and right as she continued to walk. She tried to find Anthony and succeeded. He was standing near the store selling home decor on the other side of the arcade.

He was talking to a woman.

Iris.

Why is Iris with Anthony?

Why is Anthony in Metro Manila?

"I think we need to go back," said Erika.

"Why?" Lories replied.

Loris looked at the direction where Erika's eyes were fixed, and she realized why Erika was not moving at all.

"Hey, it's OK. I think I need new Santa Claus decor in the house. We can go back to where we were earlier," said Loris while pointing to the direction they had been.

Erika was very thankful to Loris. Her best friend has always been with her.

And right now, when Erika seemed rooted to her spot,

it was Loris who ushered her in the opposite direction. They continued to walk until they couldn't see Anthony and Iris anymore.

They stopped in the store that sells Santa Claus items, big and small. Loris bought a Santa figurine half the size of Erika.

Erika stood beside a big Santa Claus statue, and she asked Loris to take a picture of her together with it.

Something good for her to remember for this day.

Especially that Erika was wearing her pink t-shirt with the word princess in front. This was a gift she received from a friend at work.

Because she wanted to remember her visit in the arcade as a happy time, most especially as she was surrounded by colorful, vibrant, and happy things.

And Christmas is near!

And with good old Santa, it would be a perfect picture of something nice for her to remember on that trip.

Erika thought that Santa was funny.

The Santa statue had its finger in his lips on a hush gesture. It is as if he was hushing Erika to be quiet. To not say a thing.

So, Erika smiled and kept her mouth shut as Loris took their picture. Erika whispered to Santa that she needs better Christmas presents this year.

Back at her place, while sipping her tea, Erika's mind can't stop thinking of what she saw. She can't unsee what she already saw even if she tries, and that was Anthony with Iris.

Did I make a mistake of leaving without saying hello to Anthony?

Was that a right decision?

Erika has no idea what happened between her and Anthony. For the past six years, their communication became less and less as the months and years passed by.

She feels that they just have drifted apart in a sense.

Erika tries to remember the conversation she had with Loris after the Dapitan episode. Before they went back to Loris' new apartment in East Avenue, also in Quezon City, they went to the nearest coffee shop to take a rest and have some refreshments.

"I can't believe it! Anthony and Iris, together! Here, in METRO MANILA!" Loris exclaimed.

Erika stayed quiet.

She just listened to Loris.

"Do you think they are back together? I mean, in a relationship again?" Loris continued.

"I don't know," replied Erika simply.

Loris looked at Erika and studied her face. Loris tried to read her reaction.

"That's it? Why are you so calm? Don't you feel anything? Have you gotten over your feelings for Anthony?" Loris fired Erika with so many questions.

This irritated Erika.

She rolled her eyes before replying.

"What do you want me to say? Anthony can do whatever he wants or has been doing. And so am I. That's why we didn't promise anything to each other."

"Actually, that's what I don't understand." Loris started again.

"Until now, everything between you and Anthony is

vague for me. Anthony admittedly said through his letter that he loves you, and you love him too. Anthony didn't want to promise anything because it would be unfair for you and him, as you both were chasing your dreams separately at that time. And now the chasing is over. You are now a lawyer, and so is Anthony. So, why can't there be a happy ending for you and him then?" Loris said in a long monologue.

"It is not hard to understand, Loris, if you will consider many other factors. You forgot about the fact that there has been six years of silence between us. There are many things that can happen or maybe already happened during those times. Feelings changed. People met other people. Circumstances are different now than before. They said that absence makes the heart go fonder. Maybe! But sometimes it can weaken also the emotions one feels." Erika explained.

"Are you saying that Anthony might have a change of feelings for you, Erika?" Loris asked.

She didn't let Erika answer right away as Loris continued, "Because I know that you still love him. All these years, you have never been in a relationship. It is not because no one is interested in you, but rather the opposite. I think, deep in your heart, you are still waiting for Anthony. Your brain may be telling you that everything is OK, but your heart is telling otherwise," said Loris.

Loris raised her eyebrow to Erika, daring her to contradict what she had just said.

Erika contemplated what she would say next.

Sometimes, Erika felt that she didn't have to explain how she feels or what's on her mind, especially when it comes to Anthony.

But here I am, sitting opposite Loris, and I am doing exactly like that, explaining myself to her.

Ironic!

Or maybe pathetic!

"What I am saying is, why can't we just let things be? There are no broken promises. He owes me nothing, and neither do I with Anthony. I love him still, but sometimes love isn't enough. I won't be living my life revolving around him. And Anthony, too, shouldn't be doing that!" Erika said.

And she meant it.

Loris didn't press Erika more.

They finished their refreshments and went back to Loris' apartment. Erika helped Loris carry all the decorations she bought back to her apartment. And after that, Erika went back to Makati.

And now Erika is alone again in her condo. She enjoys her cup of tea and the peace of being on her own.

She has many workloads to finish, but she hasn't started yet because Erika is busy thinking about mostly Anthony.

Erika remembers texting Anthony as often as she could during those six years but took into consideration that he might be busy just like she was.

Once in a while, he would reply.

The last text message Anthony sent her was to congratulate her on passing the bar exam.

Congratulations, Erika! Or should I say Atty. Erika Manalo? I am so very proud of you and I miss you. Good luck ahead!

See you when I see you! ☺

She replied to thank him and wish him best of luck, too, on his studies.

Thank you! Still Erika. So call me Erika.
Good luck to you, too. Soon, you'll be
Atty. Anthony Jay Borja. Miss you too! ☺

Anthony didn't reply to her last text, so she sent a poem to him via email two months later.

Subject: Nothing has ever changed

Anthony,

Nothing has ever changed

You and I are friends
In many ways and in every sense
The day starts and ends
But nothing has ever changed!

You went somewhere else
And here, at home, I stayed
Separately, we chased our dreams
But nothing has ever changed!

The gap between you and me
Is growing wider by the second
We are not getting any younger
But nothing has ever changed!

Alone, I sit on this wooden bench
The one that once belonged to us
Looking far beyond the distance
And still, nothing has ever changed!

No message, just a poem.

She waited that week for a reply, but none came.

Erika even remembers waiting for months for a reply from Anthony, but still none came.

None.

No reply.

Not even when Erika sent Anthony a text to congratulate him when he passed the bar exam.

Yes, Erika knows that he is now a lawyer like her. She saw his name on the list of bar passers in the newspaper, and she saw it on the website of the Supreme Court of the Philippines.

She then decided to give up on waiting for a reply.

Chapter 19

"Atty. Manalo, the driver is waiting for you in front of the building," says Lizzie.

Lizzie is Erika's very efficient office assistant. And today, Lizzie is reminding her of the appointment she has to attend to at half past two o'clock.

But Erika is still not used to being called an attorney even, after a year.

It feels surreal.

She actually preferred being called Erika.

However, it is their company policy to address everyone accordingly.

Outside of the office, though, Erika asked Lizzie to call her Erika, just Erika.

Erika goes out of her office, takes the elevator to the ground floor and walks out of the building. She sees right away the company driver.

They drive from Makati to Quezon City. Erika is going to a meeting in one of the government agencies in Quezon City.

She is not the one who is supposed to be in the meeting, but at the last minute, her colleagues can't make it. Erika was asked to attend the meeting instead. This is in relation to some cases involving their employees and their social benefits.

But before that, she will get her birth certificate with a *red ribbon* in the National Statistics Office (NSO), which Erika will use for her visa applications.

The BPO company where she works is sending Erika to the USA for two months.

Erika's time at the NSO goes smoothly.

She still has thirty minutes before her meeting with some agency officials in their central office. It takes only a couple of minutes for Erika to reach the 12-story building of the government agency where her meeting will commence from the NSO.

Erika asks the receptionist the direction to the canteen. She will use the remaining time there. It is a big building, and she doesn't want to waste time roaming around just to find it.

Better ask.

The receptionist directs her to the 3rd floor. When Erika reaches the canteen, she orders a sandwich and soda.

Erika is on her way to the vacant table she saw earlier when she hears someone call her name. At least she heard 'Erika' and now she is assuming it was her.

Erika looks around.

And there he is, walking towards her, Anthony!

What is he doing here?

Is fate playing with me again?

Erika still can't believe that she is standing face to face with Anthony right now.

Of all places!

Why here?

She will have a meeting in about twenty minutes, and they do not have much time.

"Hello, Erika. I never expected to see you here," says Anthony after a little while.

"Hi. Me, either." Erika replies.

"What brings you here?" asks Anthony.

They sit while they continue their pleasantries.

After an emotional period between them, they are back to being formal. Erika feels like they are now strangers with each other.

"I have a meeting on the 8th floor. I am just using some of my time before I go up there. And you?" Erika says.

She looks at her watch to check that she still has time. She only has 14 minutes.

"I work here. I started recently," says Anthony.

Anthony stares at Erika as he usually does every time he is with her. Erika, on the other hand, looks at her watch again.

Anthony notices Erika's discomfort, so he takes his wallet and gets what seems to be a calling card. Anthony takes his ballpoint pen from his dress jacket and writes something at the back of the card.

"I know you are in a hurry. Here are my new numbers and emails. I wrote at the back my personal number and email. Please call me or send me a text message when you are done with your meeting." Anthony says.

Erika takes the card from Anthony and puts it in her bag. She promises to send a text.

They both stand up and walk towards the elevator. Anthony accompanies her to the 8th floor, where Erika is heading.

"Thank you," says Erika and exits the elevator while Anthony presses the number 10 inside.

Erika's meeting went well, and she was able to

accomplish the task that needs to be done.

She promised Anthony that she would send him a text or call him after the meeting.

Erika calls Anthony while she's in the car on the way back to Makati and tells him that she needs to be back in her office. Anthony understands and says that he will call her later that evening.

When Erika ends the call, she saves Anthony's number.

And later that evening, as Anthony said he would call her, he did.

Erika's phone rings.

She had changed her ringing tone last year to the standard tone available in the Android phone she's using. She looks at her phone and sees Anthony's name flashing.

Erika answers the call.

She and Anthony talks but not so long. She has a very early meeting tomorrow at work and she needs to finalize the report she will be presenting.

After Erika ends the call, she goes to her room and takes the notebook where she writes most of her poems.

She reads the poem she wrote last year.

The Song

I find myself attuned
to the lyrics of a song.
As it plays gently
while I walk alone.

I sway to the music
As my heart beats.
It carries me somewhere
In the place of my dreams.

I enjoy my swaying
to its mellow rhythm.
It gives me peace
and wonderful feelings.

Maybe tomorrow she will write another about what she is feeling now.

The question is will I send it to Anthony?

She doesn't know.

Anthony knows nothing about what is playing on her mind and what her heart is feeling right at this moment. She doesn't know either what's going on in his mind.

Erika is not sure if their meeting earlier today is any indication that fate is playing tricks with them again.

Because, as usual, no one has ever said the word 'goodbye'.

Not even when they ended the call.

Chapter 20

Two and a half months later....

"Why are you always in a bad mood these days?" Juris asked.

It is Friday, and Anthony is out with Juris. They are drinking beer in a popular bar within Makati area. He sent a text to Erika if she wanted to be with them, while Juris did the same to Loris.

Unfortunately, both received no reply.

He tried calling, but his call went to voicemail. It is always the case for the last two months.

Voicemail!

It is not a good feeling reading the last message he got from Erika, but more so when Erika is not taking any of his calls.

Anthony can't blame his cousin for noticing his behavior these past two months. He doesn't know what to do anymore. Anthony knows that it is his fault after all.

Anthony had tried to distance himself from Erika so he could concentrate on his studies. His loneliness and longing for Erika during those years away from her were making havoc to Anthony's peace of mind.

He couldn't concentrate. That was why Anthony decided not to communicate as often as he would like.

It was Anthony's hope that Erika would still wait for him and that she would understand. But Anthony guesses that he was wrong. He should have been more straight-forward with her than being vague.

And now Erika seems so distant.

When he accidentally met Erika in his workplace, he almost couldn't believe it.

Fate!

He always believes in destiny!

Anthony can still feel the bond and the feelings between them. There is something that maybe has changed between them, but Anthony knows that their feelings for each other have not.

He just needs to figure it out.

As Anthony read the last message from Erika, or the last poem in this case, there was a hint of hurt and accusations in it.

And he can't blame her.

Erika just actually wrote what happened between them in that poem. He is now up to him to make it right again.

But how?

Erika doesn't want to talk to him.

She is in fact ignoring him!

Anthony takes his mobile phone from his pocket. He opens his email and searches for something. When he finds it, he shows it to Juris for him to read.

"What is this?" Juris asked.

"Just read." Anthony replied.

The goodbye that never was

We never really said goodbye
You just said until next time
All the while I just waited and cried
For you are the one in my heart

Where you are I have no clue
You never bother to send a note or two
Your silence is breaking my heart
I don't know if I can even survive

My young heart heals with time
Though broken it is not shattered
At least now I can manage to smile
Show everyone my heart is prime

However much I really tried to forget
Destiny is pulling a string like a magnet
You show up after years of incognito
Is testing my patience and own bravado

Do I need to hear what you have to say?
Now that I am moving on from this gray
Can you put together the broken segments?
Parts of me that only you can amend

"That's why you are always in a foul mood." Juris said.

Anthony told Juris everything that had happened between him and Erika.

Juris is the only person Anthony knows that can help him; the only one he trusts right now who knows the story between them.

"You are an idiot! Don't you know that?" Juris accused him.

Anthony accepted that.

"I know. That is why I want to do it right." Anthony says.

"Look, read this," says Juris afterwards when Anthony didn't say anything.

Juris shows him the text message he received from Loris earlier when Anthony seemed drifting.

"Is this right? Erika is in the US?" Anthony asks.

"It seems so. Maybe that is why she isn't replying." Juris answers.

"Did Loris say how long Erika will be there?" Anthony asked.

"Only a couple of months. Erika is expected to return a week from now," says Juris.

This gives him hope.

Anthony plans on winning Erika back.

He will woo her the way Erika deserves, and nothing less.

He just hopes that it is not yet late!

Chapter 21

Is destiny pulling the strings between me and Anthony?

Erika finds herself asking that question.

She is in a first-class seat beside her colleague, Alden. They had been to the USA for a two-month business trip and are now on their way back home to the Philippines.

Erika dated Alden before.

But there were no *sparks* between them.

Erika wasn't thrilled at all.

So, Erika decided it was not worth continuing. She doesn't want to use her energy for something for which there's no future.

They are good friends and colleagues, anyway.

During these two months, Anthony has been calling her and sending messages.

Erika didn't reply to any of them.

She was so focused at work that she didn't want to lose her control.

Anthony called Erika that evening while she was nursing her heart. It was the same day Erika saw him with Iris at the Dapitan arcade.

Erika found herself in turmoil again.

To help her deal with it, Erika penned what she felt and thought in that last poem.

Erika then sent the poem to Anthony, and after that,

Erika stopped communicating with him.

Not even now.

How long can she do that?

Erika doesn't know.

She misses Anthony so much, but she needs to control her emotions first. Most especially when her work needs her full and sharp attention to details.

For now, Erika will hold on until there's nothing to hold on to anymore.

She is not even sure if Anthony would have called her if they didn't accidentally meet. He has been in Manila for quite a while, and yet he didn't inform her.

But the connection between them still sizzles. Erika felt that in their last meeting.

Their accidental meeting two and a half months ago, though it was brief, confirmed that Erika still loves Anthony. The connection between her and Anthony is still there. The sizzling feeling is always present.

My goodness!

She almost couldn't trust herself to walk towards the elevator that day because her legs were wobbling.

This roller coaster ride that Erika feels she has been on for a long time is tiring her emotionally.

Erika thought that she was already in control and already moving on; fate was coming and dangling something she always wanted in front of her.

Testing her bravado!

The dynamic of their friendship is not what it used to be. Things have changed. But it doesn't mean that Erika has forgotten Anthony or her feelings for him.

Erika knows that deep in her heart, she will never ever forget about Anthony.

He will forever be in my heart!

But that doesn't mean that her life will revolve around him.

Anthony might be her first love, but maybe he will not be her last.

Maybe.

Who knows?

The End

The gray between us

A dusk of pale tangerine
Envelopes us as we sit
Staring right at the horizon
Filled with unspoken emotion

The calmness of the sea
And the serenity of the sky
Are giving no clues about
The storm in a fragile heart

Afraid to say what we feel
The summer wind sends a chill
Not ready to go the distance
And ruin what we have now

In the stillness of time
Our friendship goes a mile
Clouds above our sky
And the gray between us!

Acknowledgement

I would like to thank everyone who inspires me, motivates me, believes in me, supports me, and guides me in pursuing my dream of writing. The journey became easier because of your continuous support and encouragement.

To Dr. Simplicio P. Alba, for his unending support and encouragement since my "Tag-araw" days and for opening the door that gave way to my writing journey.

To Dr. Victoria Sarmiento-Yoo, and Fr. Jhun Bolo, OP, for giving me words of encouragement, and including me and my family in their prayers.

My heartfelt thanks to my family and friends (most especially to Resi, Nelma, Jho, and Nancy Joy), who journeyed with me as I weaved the story decades ago. Your willingness to hear all the little stories behind this one made the journey more exciting and bearable.

I would also like to extend my gratitude to a smart and talented young girl, Deudonne Mireo 'Rio' Orpia, for capturing the essence of the story and bringing it to life by making the cover image of this book.

I want to acknowledge also and extend my gratitude to Poetry Planet Book Publishing House for giving me this opportunity to publish my first short novel "The Gray between Us."

I am forever thankful to my beloved son, Jan Alexander, for gracing my life with so much love, happiness, purpose, inspiration, and for helping me choose "Anthony" as the name of my guy character.

And of course, to my husband, Jan-Helge, for his love, care, patience, and support every single day.

Above all, I thank our Almighty God for blessing me with everything and everyone I need in my life.

About the author

Alona Teodoro Simonsen is a licensed professional teacher in the Philippines even before moving to Europe. She has more than a decade of teaching experience in the Philippines and abroad. She was interested in theater and other cultural activities back when she was still living in the Philippines. During the COVID-19 pandemic, she used online platforms to continuously participate in ARTIST, Inc programs such as Likhandula International Arts Exchange and Collaboration. She is currently an active member of ARTIST Inc Abroad. Alona is busy balancing her family life, and her work. During her «me time», Alona loves to watch sports and write poems, essays, and short stories.

The Gray between Us is her first published short novel.

She had self-published one poetry book in English with the title *The Heart's Journey: The path I always dreamed of* and co-authored the poetry book in Filipino entitled *Tilamsik ng Diwa: 100 Tula Para sa Iyo*.

Above all, Alona is a devoted wife and a loving mother to their child.

Facebook: My Literary Journey: the writer in me

Instagram: @alonasimonsen

Other Books from the Author

The Heart's Journey: The path I always dreamed of is a collection of poems, essays, and short stories.

Tilamsik ng Diwa: 100 Tula Para sa Iyo is a poetry book in Filipino.

www.ingramcontent.com/pod-product-compliance
Lightning Source LLC
LaVergne TN
LVHW050536160826
845677LV00011B/2062